THE CHARCOAL HORSE

Also by Edward Loomis:

END OF A WAR

THE CHARCOAL HORSE

a novel by

EDWARD LOOMIS

ALAN SWALLOW, *Denver*

"But, Sir, how can you call the kettle black, when you are as black as the kettle is?"

"Indeed, Sir, I find it very easy; for in spite of the fact that I am a black pot, he is a very black kettle."

CHAPTER ONE

Thomas Bird Gillespie was neither awake nor asleep. He lay on his right side with his arms locked in front of his chest. He was wrapped from head to foot in a single blanket, one man among eighty men who slept or tried to sleep on the stone floor. He was less fortunate than the others only in that he was nearest to the doors. He could see the screen door that opened on the hall; he could feel the winter wind that came in under the big outside door at the end of the hall: the wind passed under the sill of the outside door, not pausing at the locks, and on through the screen door into the room. The eighty men rolled restlessly in the wind; the draft was in their dreams and none escaped it.

Gillespie tried to sleep by locking his eyes shut, but the gesture was futile. The cold floor and the cold wind prevented sleep; shivering, Gillespie was a bulwark for all the men in the room. He protected the men in the center and he envied them all. He rolled in a slow fit, seeing the doors, feeling the wind, seeing the barred windows; his prisoned body fitted itself to the prison chills with a simple organic desperation. He longed for distractions.

He tried to find shapes in the darkness above his head, but his vision penetrated the darkness without finding any obstruction; he did not look at the windows. In the room with him, he could smell the men who slept and he could hear their noises, but he could find nothing to attract him. He was pleased at eleven o'clock when one of the guards brought in a new prisoner; he hoped for diversion. He hid his head under the blanket, leaving a gap for his eyes, and watched.

The guard opened the big door carefully; he rattled the key in the lock and listened as the key slid solidly home: the lock fell open before him and he entered. He beckoned the man behind him to follow:

"There it is," he said. "Here's your home." The guard walked up to the screen door and flashed his light across the room, looking along the beam. He nodded his head slowly as the light picked out the round sleeping forms. Gillespie ducked his head back into the blanket as the light passed him; he saw the light flicker past and he moved his head slowly forward again.

The guard dropped the beam of light to the floor in front of him and turned to the man who had followed him in. "Have you got a blanket?" he asked.

"No," the man said. "No blanket."

The guard lifted his light to the man's chest. "You're supposed to have a blanket," he said. "What did you do with it?"

"I never had a blanket," the man said. "They must have forgotten it."

"Somebody forgot it," the guard said. "They're supposed to issue the blanket before they send you over here. Jesus." The guard turned the light upon his wrist watch. "Eleven o'clock," he said. "The supply sergeant is probably asleep: you'll have to get the blanket in the morning." He swept the beam of light again into the room. Gillespie, watching, did not flinch; he held his head steady. The guard grinned a little as he looked out into the room.

"Maybe one of these guys will let you share his," he said.

The man beside him looked into the room along the beam of light. "That's all right," he said. "I can sleep standing."

The guard turned away as if he had not heard what the man had said. He tucked his flashlight under his left armpit and stepped to the screen door. He started to fumble with his keys and then he stopped; slowly he stopped his fingers in their fumbling with the keys, retrieved the flashlight, and turned around again to the man behind him.

"What was that again?" he asked. He bent forward, squinting in the darkness above the light in his hand; the flashlight scattered brightness through the narrow hall. The man behind him moved away from the wall. In a clear voice he said:

"I can sleep standing."

The guard played the beam slowly from the man's face down to

his feet, as if in inspection. Then, pointing the light at the big outside door, he brushed past the man.

"Stay here," he said.

He went to the big door and pulled it open; he leaned out
above the sill. "Anse," he called. "Hey Anse. Come on over
here."

Gillespie lifted his head but he could not see the door; he heard
someone answer from outside: "What is it? Trouble?"

"No trouble," the first guard called from the door. "Just something I want you to see." He gestured with the light. "In here,"
he said. He turned the light back upon the man in the hall,
centering the beam on the man's middle; he stood back to allow
the guard Anse to enter. Then they both followed the beam into
the hall.

"Well, what is it?" the guard Anse asked. "What do you want,
Shannon?"

"Something to see," Shannon answered. He gestured. "That
right there: it's a man who can sleep standing." Shannon
laughed a little as he spoke; the laughter moved quietly in his
throat. "That's all," he said. "Just a man who can sleep standing."

For a moment, Anse said nothing. He moved a little closer to
the man in the light and then stopped.

"Ah, what the hell," he said. "What is this?"

"Don't you get it?" Shannon asked.

"No, I don't get it." The guard Anse turned, as if to leave. "I
don't get it," he repeated.

"Then wait a minute," Shannon said. The laughter was gone
out of his throat; he lifted his hand to bar the way. "Just wait a
minute," he said. He turned toward the man he had brought in,
planted his feet, and said: "Tell us again."

The man waited; he stood with both hands at his sides. He
looked down at the beam of light.

"Go on," Shannon said impatiently, lifting the light. "Tell us
how you can sleep."

The man hesitated; Gillespie saw his lips move a little as if he
were choosing words. Then he said, in the same manner as
before: "I can sleep standing."

9

Shannon turned triumphantly away.

"You see?" he asked the guard Anse. "He says he can sleep standing. Now how do you like that?"

The guard Anse looked quietly at him for a moment, and then he brushed the retaining hand aside. "I don't see nothing," he said. "I'm going back to the post." He stepped suddenly past Shannon and walked to the door. At the door, he paused. "Why don't you let the guy alone?" he asked quietly. He waited for an answer; hearing nothing, he went on: "I'll see you later, Shannon," he said. He closed the big door behind him.

For almost a minute, Shannon did not move nor speak; then he turned again to the man behind him. "That's too bad," he said. "That bastard don't care about anything." He stood uncertainly, playing with the switch on the flashlight: the beam went on and off, piercing the darkness. "But I do," he said suddenly. "What's your name, man?" he asked. He had the beam again on the man's middle.

"Osgood," the man answered.

"Osgood," Shannon repeated. "That's easy to remember. What's your first name?"

"Benjamin."

"Benjamin," Shannon repeated. "Benjamin Osgood." He paused, as if he were trying to think of something more to say. "And where are you from, Osgood? What's your unit?"

Osgood for a long time had not moved. With the last question, he shifted his feet, and turned his right arm away from his body. "Infantry," Osgood answered. His voice had changed; his voice had an edge of pride.

Gillespie, hearing the sudden irritation in Osgood's voice, pushed his head out of the blanket, and strained his eyes to see more clearly past the beam of light; he saw Shannon lift the light and step back one step. When he spoke, there was uncertainty in his voice. "Then that's it," he said. "You're an infantry soldier. I asked what unit?"

Osgood did not answer; he twisted his right arm, as if to relieve it from the cold. He looked steadily at the guard Shannon.

10

"Come on!" Shannon said angrily. "I asked you a question. What's your unit?"

"The First Division," Osgood answered quietly; his voice was almost inaudible: the last word dwindled off his tongue into silence. Then, before Shannon could say anything more, he said: "The First goddamn Infantry Division: try another question." He lifted his right hand suddenly to the back of his neck; he kneaded the muscles in the back of his neck. His whole upper body writhed with the motion. With his head down, he asked, in a sharp question: "What are you getting at for Christ's sake?"

Shannon lifted the beam of light in a quick reaction of surprise, and crouched forward, cocking his shoulders.

"What are you getting at?" Osgood asked again. Dropping his hand to his side again, he straightened. "It's late," he said. "You don't have to do this." He lifted his head and looked at Shannon above the light. Shannon straightened with him: the tension flowed away as quickly as it had come. The flashlight wavered in Shannon's hand.

"All I wanted was an answer," he said. "I asked a question and got an answer." He waited a moment, and then he said: "You got no complaint about that, do you?"

Osgood shook his head. "No," he said. "No complaint about that."

"All right then," Shannon said genially. He turned the light away from Osgood toward the screen door. "Let's get on with it." Following the light, Shannon moved to the screen door. Holding the flashlight under his armpit, he selected another key, and set it toward the lock. Gillespie withdrew his head when he saw Shannon move; he heard Shannon breathing heavily above him, and he heard the key scrape twice against the lock before it clicked home into the keyhole. Gillespie rolled away from the door as he heard the door open inward, but he could not move far enough; the door in its sweep bounced against him and rebounded a little toward Shannon. Gillespie stuck his head out of the blanket, directly into the bright beam of light; he blinked and started to rise.

"Come on get up," Shannon said to him. "Get up and let this

11

man in." Shannon turned to Osgood. "Here you are," he said. He stood back to let Osgood pass.

Osgood walked slowly past him into the room, edging around the door. Gillespie, holding his blanket like a skirt around his middle, moved awkwardly away, watching Shannon close the door. With the door closed and the lock fixed, Shannon stood back and turned his light upon the two men standing inside. He nodded his head.

"Now you're home," he said. He turned the light upon Gillespie; he scrutinized him carefully before he spoke. "You," he said. "What's your name?" He fidgeted with the light to accentuate his question.

"Gillespie," the answer came. Gillespie shivered and wrapped the blanket closer about his body.

"All right then, Gillespie," Shannon said. "How about sharing your blanket with this man?" He flicked the light upon Osgood. "This is a new man who has no blanket."

"Why sure," Gillespie answered. "I'll be glad to."

"That's fine," Shannon answered. "That's what I like to hear. Do it now."

"I'll do it," Gillespie said.

Shannon turned his head toward Osgood. "You see?" he said. "I didn't mean nothing with it; I was just asking questions."

Osgood nodded his head. "I see," he said.

"I don't want you men to get me wrong," Shannon said. "You know I just work here." He waited for an answer; getting none, he continued: "I got a job, that's all." He grinned along the light, and moved forward to the door. "Now is everything all right in there?" he asked.

"Everything's all right," Osgood answered.

"All right then," Shannon said. He stepped away. "Good night then. Good night, you sons of bitches." He snapped the light out; turning in darkness, he stepped toward the square blackness of the big door. His laughter filtered back from the closing door into the dark hall and on into the dark room; the locks snapped shut upon a remnant of his laughter.

The two men stood listening to the laughter die away in the

big room, Osgood alert and angry, Gillespie cold in his blanket and worried at his involvement in the trouble. Osgood moved first; he stepped toward the door and, turning, leaned his shoulders against it.

"Well I'll be damned," he said. He looked toward Gillespie and laughed a little. "What do you think of that?"

Gillespie gathered his blanket higher around his shoulders, wrapped it tight, and sat down. "I don't think much of it," he said. "What should I think about it?" He stretched out on the floor again; he did not look at Osgood.

Osgood looked down in mild surprise; he slipped his hands into his pockets and settled himself against the frame of the screen door. "That's all right," he said. "I can't figure it either."

Gillespie slowly stretched backward to the floor, watching Osgood and waiting for the request for the sharing of the blanket. Behind him, he heard the steady sound of sleep in the room; he thought again of his irritation at being caught near the door for the cold night. He looked up again at Osgood and saw that Osgood had relaxed against the door; his figure seemed to telescope into itself. Gillespie was surprised: when the guard had spoken about sharing the blanket, he had offered an advantage to Osgood; and now Osgood had refused it. Gillespie laughed a little, the silent intestinal shiver of laugh used by secretive people in public places; but he did it poorly: Osgood turned. For a moment, he looked down at Gillespie; he turned his head away when he was done as if he had seen enough. Gillespie, watching from within his blanket, felt the rejection. In his embarrassment, he shoved the blanket back from his head and sat up. He lifted his right hand toward Osgood.

"Soldier," he said. "You by the door."

Osgood braced himself straight with a quick quiver of shoulder; he stood easily, watching Gillespie. "You want me?" he asked.

"You," Gillespie answered. "I have a blanket if you want a part of it; I remember now what the guard said."

"Thanks," Osgood said. He lifted one hand from a pocket, and waved it away from his hip. "It's all right," he went on. "It's like I told the guard: I can sleep standing."

"You're welcome to it," Gillespie said. "I'd be glad to share it."

Osgood shook his head. "No," he said. "I'll try it on my feet tonight."

Gillespie rolled back to the floor. "All right," he said. "I asked you."

"And I'll remember it," Osgood said. "Thanks very much for the offer." He dropped his hand into his pocket again, and settled to the wall. Gillespie stretched out, feeling uncomfortable but satisfied that he had obeyed the order; he was pleased that he would be able, if necessary, to satisfy Shannon's questions, but he was disturbed by Osgood's easy rejection of his offer. He decided scornfully that it had been pride that caused the rejection. Looking at Osgood, he thought idly and without direction of the problem of pride; and when his thoughts wandered, he made no effort to bring them back. After a time, he turned his back on Osgood and stretched his body to the floor; and before he remembered to turn again to see if Osgood was still standing, his eyes closed. Before he slept, he heard a train whistle three times in the distance; wondering where the train was going, he thought of the cities he knew: he thought of London, blacked out and all dark in the night, but he could not summon sharp images; only the pattern of all the streets, and his memory of the smell of fog. When he slept, he slept soundly.

CHAPTER TWO

Gillespie woke quickly in the morning on the steady blast of a whistle; the whistle carried him to his feet before he could clean the night's sediment from his eyes.

He stepped automatically back from the screen door and saw the tall figure of Sgt. Cann; before he turned away, he saw the Sergeant's cheeks popped outward with his effort: the sound of the whistle shattered the heavy rhythmic sound of sleep in the room.

"Get up goddammit," the Sergeant said, lowering the whistle from his mouth. "Get up get up," he roared. "You have three minutes to make this formation."

The men behind Gillespie began to move; they came at him in an amorphous rush, charging and moving faster as they approached the door, and Gillespie turned with them, toward the door, without thinking. The men behind him carried him on ahead of them, but he could not avoid their smell: they carried about their bodies the stiff powerful smell of sweat; they had a complicated urinary smell in the narrow hall. Gillespie gasped as he stepped outside the building into the cold air, and his relief at escaping the smells of the men who followed him dissolved in the fluid sharp cold that met him at the door. He sucked in one lungful of the moist air and then held his breath as he moved to his position in the formation.

He ran from the barracks to his left, following prison commands: he ran because he and all the prisoners ran everywhere; and he ran to his left because his place in the formation was set inflexibly five yards to the left of the front corner of the barracks. He turned quietly to wait the coming of the guides who would set the direction of the lines, and he saw Osgood moving up behind him. The mass of men came on behind Osgood and Osgood was lost in the swirl of moving men; who moved by habit and on the encouragement of the guard Shannon, who

15

stood on the top step outside the building. In a loud voice, Shannon drove the men before him; the four platoons shaped themselves suddenly under his angry urging.

Gillespie, at the end of his rank, felt someone moving in beside him, to his left, and he turned to protest; he turned and saw Osgood settling himself slowly into a position of attention.

"Are you sure this is your place?" Gillespie asked. "I'm supposed to be the last man in this rank."

"This is as good as any place," Osgood answered. "They haven't assigned me a regular place yet."

Gillespie opened his mouth to speak against this irregularity, but he heard Shannon's voice approaching from the rear, and he held his comments, uneasy at seeing a departure from the routine, but afraid to speak again within hearing of the guard. He listened to the sounds of the movement to the formation; across the quadrangle, he heard the other companies of prisoners coming down to their places. There was almost no sound now: only the voices of the guards, and above all the voices, the voice of the guard Shannon.

As Shannon moved to the front of the company, Gillespie straightened, although he was almost out of sight in the rear rank. Once a guard had caught him in a slouch, and since that time, Gillespie had been wary and correct. Now and then, to preserve his personal honor, he let one knee relax; but that was all. He paid no attention to Osgood; he watched Shannon move to the front of the company.

Shannon stepped slowly, carrying his rifle loosely in his right hand, looking over his shoulder for Sgt. Cann. He turned indecisively in front of the company and looked up at the door to the barracks; some of the men in the company turned with him, watching, and a slow stir of sound began to rustle through the ranks. Hearing it, Shannon looked down at the company.

"Attention!" he shouted uneasily. "Attention!"

The noise stopped momentarily with the order, and then began again as Shannon looked again at the door. Gillespie did not turn his head, but he wondered at the Sergeant's absence. Across the quadrangle, he could hear the roll being called in the other com-

16

panies; idly, and with a mild expectancy, he hoped that the Sergeant would be delayed so that he would be unable to complete his roll call in time for the report to the battalion officer of the day; he hoped for anything that might puncture the Sergeant's confidence and provide him with diversion and laughter during the day. He watched Shannon; after an uneasy interval of thirty seconds, he saw Shannon stiffen suddenly.

"Attention!" Shannon called. "Attention!"

Disappointedly, hearing new confidence in Shannon's voice, Gillespie realized that the Sergeant must have come out of the barracks; in the silence that followed Shannon's call, he heard the Sergeant's steps behind him. The Sergeant passed between the first and second platoons, and out in front of the company where Gillespie could see him; he moved deliberately, but more quickly than usual. He checked the company into a strict attention as he turned; his heels smacked together to punctuate the command.

"Attention!" Then he called the roll. He read the names from his list by the light of his flashlight; he turned the light upon each man as he answered. The light, searching out each man in turn, illuminated the power of the Sergeant; the light showed each prisoner his position with unanswerable clarity. The Sergeant read each name carefully.

"Emmet, Erne, Falaschi, Felix, Ferber, Garber."

Gillespie stirred a little as the penetrating easy voice came closer to his own name; he started to think about his answer. He turned over in his mind the different ways of answering: with confidence, with cockiness, with anger, with meekness, with firmness; and with the mixed meekness and firmness which attracted the least attention. He enjoyed the roll calls; he was able to acknowledge in public his private vanity: the feeling that he was yet a man bearing a name. He knew the names in the list which immediately preceded his own. Garber, Garfield, Gebhardt, Gibbs; the rhythm enforced remembrance. When the Sergeant called his name, he was ready.

"Gillespie?"

"Here."

The answer was right; the next name, Gruenberg, came quickly: the light did not linger in his eyes. He breathed more easily, glad that he had received no special attention, and he listened with a lessened attention to the rest of the roll call; he waited for the name, Osgood, but until the end he did not hear it. The Sergeant read the familiar list, stopped, and then spoke to Shannon; he looked up and called out a final name.

"Osgood?"

"Here," Osgood answered in a firm solid voice.

"Osgood," the Sergeant went on, "you'll come see me after this formation is over. I want to talk to you a little bit."

"All right, Sergeant," Osgood answered.

The Sergeant looked up for a moment, as if he were memorizing the answer, and then he turned, in the quick military shuffle, to face away from the platoons to give his report; he gave his report loudly. When the call came from across the square, he answered swiftly, pausing a little on each word for emphasis, but hurrying through the statement.

"C Company all present and accounted for, Sir!"

Gillespie, hearing the rich vigor of the Sergeant's voice, thought a little bitterly of the obvious enjoyment the Sergeant found in giving the report, in performing the duty of an officer; he thought angrily of Lt. Camber, the company officer, still in bed and warm between sheets, who by his absence had permitted the Sergeant this pleasure.

After the report, the Sergeant turned again to the company; he inspected the lines in a brief glance from left to right, and then he centered his gaze on the second platoon.

"I've told you men the Colonel was going to inspect this barracks tomorrow," he began. "Now I'm telling you again. Before we go to breakfast, I want you men to get started. I mean I want you all to do something. I want this barracks to shine." He paused and looked from one end of the line to the other. "But there's one thing I don't want you men to touch in that barracks." The Sergeant straightened a little; in the darkness above the flashlight, Gillespie could see his head move, and he could hear the change in the Sergeant's voice.

"There's a drawing on the wall of the barracks this morning,"

18

the Sergeant said flatly. "It is an improper drawing. One of you men put that drawing on the wall in order to make a joke; but no one is going to appreciate the joke. And nobody is going to laugh at it." The Sergeant paused again; he turned his head a little to the side as if listening for noises or comments, but there was no sound. "And I want you men to leave that drawing alone; don't touch that wall." He turned to Shannon. "You'll see to that, Shannon."

Shannon nodded his head; the Sergeant waited for his words to take effect; when he spoke, his voice was calm again.

"Now here's the details for the day."

He started to read the list of work assignments. The men listened carefully, not wishing to seek attention by the necessity of asking questions later; each man wished to remain anonymous. Gillespie's name came up on the detail assigned to cleaning the Colonel's quarters. It was an easy detail and he was pleased. He was still thinking about the warm house he would work in when he got inside the barracks; the lights were on and there was a small group of men looking at the wall to the left of the door. The group broke up suddenly as Shannon came in.

"Come on, get going," Shannon said. "Get away from that wall."

Gillespie, suddenly curious, turned reluctantly away; he caught only a brief flash of black lines on the wall, and he was unable to read the inscription. Most of the men were now trying to start the cleaning; it was the required gesture. A few, seeing little to do in the big room, and afraid to move close to the picture, went directly to the latrine. Gillespie remained in the big room. He picked up a scrap of paper near the latrine, and then, searching for something else to pick up, he moved toward the screen door. Twenty feet from the door, the bright metal end of a shoelace reflected the light from the bulbs in the ceiling. Moving with a hunched and dutiful back, Gillespie walked toward the door. He bent down slowly, picked up the piece of metal, and looked up at the picture as he stood up; he gasped suddenly and then he turned away. Scraped with something like charcoal on the wall was a crude drawing of a horse with enormous hindquarters; above the drawing, there was an inscription, circled, with a heavy arrow pointing to the hindquarters of the horse: This is the horses ass Camber. The inscription was printed in capital letters.

Gillespie, turning, felt a sudden wracking impulse to laughter as he thought of Lt. Camber, now safe in bed, but soon to suffer under a general ridicule. Concealment was not possible; and before the day was out, the picture would receive the attention of the officers of the prison battalion and all the laughter of the prison. Gillespie started to shape a grin, hiding it under his hand, when he heard Shannon's voice: "You there! Get moving and get to work!"

Gillespie, startled, looked wildly over his shoulder, and caught Shannon's eye; Shannon lifted his right arm and pointed at him.

"Yes, you!" he shouted. "Get going now!"

Bobbing his head jerkily, Gillespie stepped away, toward the back of the room, already regretting his boldness in looking at the picture. Remembering Shannon's command, he suddenly felt the possibilities implicit in the picture; he realized how his laughter and the laughter of others could extend in fearful ramifications of trouble and disaster, expanding the wrath of Lt. Camber upward through echelons of anger in the prison hierarchy until it could never be called back or completely satisfied. He felt already involved in the trouble after Shannon's reprimand; he knew the prison officials could not pass by a crime of this nature; a picture as big and plain as the one on the wall.

Moving a little unsteadily, Gillespie walked toward the latrine; above him, the sound of hurrying footsteps clanged through the old flooring: he thought enviously of the warm wood flooring of the second story and contrasted it with the stone floor he walked on. He felt the cold of the stone transmitted through the damp leather of his shoes, and it reminded him that the men on the second floor would have no difficulties because of the picture on the first floor wall.

He was late getting to the latrine. The seats were all occupied, the bowls were in use; there was a rank of men before the urinal tray. Gillespie waited behind a man at a washbowl, careful always to protect his rotational turn by staying close to the man's rump. Once someone brushed him from behind, and he thought for a moment that he might have to speak for his place; but it was an accident. The man who had brushed him went on out into the main room. When Gillespie's turn came, he woke himself in a splash of cold water, and then went to stand in line before the urinal. When he was finished with that, he was ready to face the day. As he left the latrine, he saw the new man, Osgood, entering, with a face rigid and stiff with anger. Gillespie guessed that Sgt. Cann had reprimanded Osgood for his brush the night before with Shannon the guard. Gillespie grinned a little as he passed, pleased that others beside himself had troubles. For a brief instant, he forgot the set of apprehensions that centered upon the picture on the wall, in his enjoyment of Osgood's irritation and anger.

CHAPTER THREE

Gillespie worked in warmth all day in the Colonel's house; he cleaned the living room and the front hall. Sometimes when he passed a window, he stopped to look out at the men passing by: they passed the house walking fast and sometimes running, with their coatcollars wrapped about their ears, and their breath frosting the air before them. Watching them, Gillespie laughed happily and mockingly, feeling the heat from the radiators in the room envelop his body.

The Colonel's Orderly, Johnson, pleased him almost as much as the warm rooms. Johnson was remarkably neat, and he seemed happy: his face was shaved to a red bareness that reflected the light; but he addressed the prisoners on the detail pleasantly, as if they were not prisoners at all.

Gillespie's only worry fell across the picture and the words on the barracks wall. He tried to convince himself that the prison authorities would overlook the offense; but he could not persuade himself: he knew that mockery never pleased superior officers. He could imagine the fearful punishments that would be devised for the man who had made the picture, if that man were ever found; he feared that the whole company might suffer through partaking of the punishment, as by their observation of the picture they had partaken of laughter. He remembered uneasily that he himself had slept near the screen door, not twenty feet from the picture. He felt an irrational anger that he had chosen this position; he was afraid that he might have to answer questions if there were an investigation.

That night, some of his fears came home to him. When he returned to the barracks, he found that the picture had been washed from the wall. And after the evening routine of roll call and admonitions by Sgt. Cann had been completed, the Sergeant called the company to attention and stepped aside for the company officer, Lt. Camber. The Lieutenant stepped forward, waiting for a moment while surveying the company disapprovingly, and then spoke.

"I have an announcement," he said. He paused and cleared his throat. "This barracks is in trouble again."

The lines of men stirred; here and there, a man drew breath quickly in anticipation. Sgt. Cann heard the noise: "Attention," he called. "Quiet down in there."

The stir died quickly. The Lieutenant waited; when the men were entirely quiet, he went on.

"This morning," he said, "one of you men insulted me publicly on a wall of the barracks. One of you thought it was an amusing joke; but this joke was reported, properly, to the officer of the day; who in turn reported it to camp headquarters. The joke has now come to the attention of Colonel Vopel and the Colonel has ordered an investigation."

The vague stir within the company began again; there was a ripple of sound all along the line. The Sergeant, hearing the rise of noise, stepped in ahead of the Lieutenant.

"Attention," he shouted. "Attention in there!" He raised his right hand. "Goddamn it, stop that noise. Stop that noise or I'll run you twenty miles tonight." His voice ceased abruptly; he rocked back on his heels. The underground tremor of sound stopped with his voice. The men waited, suddenly apprehensive, for the Lieutenant to continue. He spoke again in a loud, angry voice.

"I'll repeat what I just told you: the Colonel has ordered an investigation. It's a serious matter as you can understand," he said. "We mean to get to the bottom of this matter."

The company of men was quiet. Gillespie could see the men ahead of him standing straighter; he felt the familiar rise of tension and fear in the men around him, and in himself.

"But for tonight," the Lt. went on, "we're holding off. We're giving you all a chance to help us out. We won't start our investigation until tomorrow at noon. If before that time the man who did this thing will come forward, the case will be closed before it starts. Do you all understand that? We are permitting the guilty man to turn himself in." The Lieutenant turned to Sgt. Cann: "Sergeant," he said quietly, "I want you to go over this with the men now; I want them to know we're serious."

"Yes, sir," the Sergeant answered. "I'll take care of it."

That night and the next morning, Gillespie, with all the men in the company, waited expectantly for something to happen. Gillespie did not think that the artist would come forward; he only hoped that he would be discovered before an investigation was started. His hopes were frustrated at reveille the next morning: Sgt. Cann angrily but quickly announced that no one had come forward; he did not linger on the subject. He immediately began an exhortation on cleaning the barracks for the Colonel's inspection; he asked for dramatic efforts. "I want it clean," he said. "I want it clean; I want that barracks clean and I'll see to it. Remember that Shannon will be watching. See that you work."

Back in the barracks, most of the men worked, or tried to work. They were hindered by the lack of tools: there were two brooms and two mops for the first floor. Gillespie picked up scraps near the door, but the floor was moderately clean, and he could find little to move. Working slowly, looking about him, he saw Osgood standing by the wall. Out of curiosity, he moved toward him. Osgood was watching another man working with a broom. While Gillespie watched, Osgood asked the man for the broom. "Here," he said. "I'll go it awhile now if you like." He grinned a little and stretched out his right hand, in a tentative motion to take the broom. The other man, an Italian named Nicoletti, shook his head.

"Naw," he said. "I'm doing all right." He turned away, and Osgood dropped his arm, and turned his head toward Gillespie. Seeing the motion, Gillespie said: "That's the way it goes." He nodded at Nicoletti. "These men like to work."

"I see that," Osgood answered. He looked at Gillespie more closely, as if he recognized the voice and face, but as if he were not certain. Gillespie nodded his head at him.

"It's me all right," he said. "I'm the one with the blanket."

Osgood stepped forward as if to look more closely. "Why sure," he said. "I thought I recognized your voice." He smiled pleasantly. "I'd like to thank you for that offer," he said, and took another step toward Gillespie.

Gillespie was about to answer when he saw Shannon coming out of the latrine toward the front of the room; Shannon was watching him. Gillespie dropped his left hand to his side and motioned with it away from his hip, toward Osgood, and then turned away to the blanket shelf. Shannon called to him as he turned. "You there," he called.

Gillespie hesitated, and then stopped; slowly he turned to face the guard.

"You there," Shannon called again. "You heard what the Sergeant said, didn't you?"

There was no proper answer to this question; Gillespie stood waiting.

"The Sergeant said he wanted you men to shine this place, and he didn't say he wanted to see anybody standing around. There's plenty to do. Do it." Short and heavy, Shannon stood looking at Gillespie. Shannon was an ordinary-looking man, and an ordinary-looking soldier. There was a blot like an inkspot on his cartridge belt, but he stood heavy with authority. "Now go on," he said. "Get a little work done." He watched as Gillespie moved toward the blanket shelf.

Gillespie walked slowly, trying to maintain his dignity; but he felt Shannon's contempt running up and down his back as he walked away.

"I won't even take your name, you're lucky," Shannon concluded.

Gillespie, watching the wall, not wanting to see Osgood or anyone else, took one of the blankets from the shelf, shook it loose, and started to fold it again. He tried to bend his entire attention upon the blanket. He refolded two more blankets before the call to breakfast.

At the breakfast formation, Osgood was assigned a permanent position; he was told off for the third platoon. He took his place beside Gillespie. Gillespie carefully avoided looking in that direction. He was still full of his humiliation, and he nourished a feeling of resentment toward Osgood because Osgood had not also been reprimanded. In the messhall, Osgood sat beside Gillespie; both in silence according to the standing order for prisoners in the messhall.

The breakfast that morning was better than usual, and Gillespie began to feel better as he ate. There was oatmeal, toast and coffee. The oatmeal was thin but hot and the coffee was strong and hot. Gillespie gulped his coffee, rinsing down the harsh phlegm from his throat, and with it the sour taste of winter morning. He drank his first cup quickly and prepared to drink a second, although sometimes the prison coffee affected his kidneys unpleasantly; in the prison, he preferred warmth to any other luxury available to him. He hurried with his meal so that he could linger over his second cup. As he picked up his cup, tasting the hot rim of the cup and the hot syrupy drink within it, he heard Osgood mutter something in his direction. Since talking was forbidden the prisoners in the messhall, he was surprised and frightened; but he turned his head a little so that he could see Osgood. He grunted at him, tentatively, to indicate that he was listening.

"Tough break," Osgood said softly. He lifted a spoonful of oatmeal to his mouth, and while he swallowed, he said: "Sorry to make trouble for you."

Gillespie nodded his head, as much to stop Osgood from saying anything further, as to agree with him. Gillespie turned his head around to the front again, and picked up his cup: he heard steps coming quickly toward him down the aisle from behind. Instantly, he thought that they were the footsteps of the Sergeant; they were heavy, but quick and buoyant. But it was Shannon the guard. He did not call out as he approached; he said nothing after he arrived until he got his breath. He stood behind Gillespie, waiting; Gillespie could feel his presence, watching; he could see the other men at the table looking beyond him with impassive faces. After they comprehended the situation, they looked straight ahead, each as if there were a puzzle or a pretty woman in the air above. Five tables away, Sgt. Cann, drinking a cup of coffee, looked up to watch.

"You again," Shannon said suddenly. He packed a measure of

26

disgust into the two words. "Stand up!" He rapped Gillespie on the shoulder with the knuckles of his left hand.

Gillespie stood up slowly, waiting for Shannon to challenge Osgood; but Shannon bent his whole attention on Gillespie. As he rose, Gillespie could feel his left knee ache where he had ripped a tendon playing football in high school; he could feel the great muscles in the thighs contract with tension; he could feel the eyes of all the men in the room rise with him. The sounds of eating declined into attention. Because the bench had been pulled toward the table after the men sat down, Gillespie could not stand straight. He was forced to bend his knees, and as a result, the line from his hips to his shoulders was crooked.

"Stand at attention!" Shannon said. He did not say it loudly; he said it with pride. Gillespie tried to straighten up by bending his knees, and he succeeded in moving the bench back a little.

"You can't stay straight an hour, can you?" Shannon said. "And you know the rule about talking in the messhall. Don't you?"

Gillespie knew the question had to be answered, but for a moment he lost his voice; he felt a trickle of sweat roll down his back inside his belt.

"Yes," he answered.

"All right then," Shannon said. "You know the rest of the rule. Get to it. Up and down in place until I tell you to stop."

As he finished speaking, Osgood twisted around in his seat and touched the guard's sleeve.

"Say," he began, and hesitated, not knowing how to address this man who had authority but no title. "Guard, I ought to tell you. . . " Before he could finish, Shannon pulled his arm away from Osgood's touch.

"No talking," he said. "I know you." To Gillespie, he said: "Come on, get started."

Then Gillespie, forgetting his hope that Osgood would be forced to share in the punishment, had to start moving as he had been directed: up and down from his seat, bending at the knees, as fast as he could move. It was a common punishment, but Gillespie had never undergone it himself; he had seen it often. He was embarrassed because he was awkward; everyone watched

27

him. The first time he bent down, he knocked a spoon from the table to the floor, and he hesitated, uncertain whether he should stop to retrieve it. Out of the corner of his eye, he saw Shannon lift his hand: he continued.

After the first five or six bends, he lost his embarrassment, and he began to have a little conscious anger as he felt the sympathy in the eyes of the other men at the table. After he had bent down fifteen times, his knees and the muscles in his legs began to stiffen. It was early morning, and there was no heat in the messhall; he was sweating inside his clothes, but the cold in the room worked on him at the same time. He thought about the way the woolen underwear would feel when he had cooled off; he thought of the cough he might take with the sudden cold when he stopped; and all the time he felt the physical agony increase. His anger increased with the agony, as he felt the justification, in his legs and back and stomach, grow larger. He felt the food he had eaten and the coffee he had drunk swirl in his stomach; with the pain in his body, he began to notice in his belly the slow turn of nausea. Each time his buttocks hit the bench, he rose more slowly. Once he slipped so that the base of his spine struck the hard wood. He was sagging when the guard spoke.

"All right," he said, "you can stop."

Gillespie rose slowly part way after he spoke, and then he dropped back. He stretched his legs under the table in a wracking luxury of relaxation. He sat without moving again until the company left the messhall. As the muscles in his stomach relaxed, the feeling of nausea, familiar and loathsome, increased. He tried to control it. He wondered vaguely how long he had been jumping in the painful dance, and he decided that it must have been more than two minutes; he could hardly believe it.

He was tired and sick and his defenses fell away. The nausea rose towards his throat, and it sucked all his attention inward; but he could feel the sympathy of the other men at the table. By the time the company stood up to leave the messhall, his muscles had recovered enough so that he could forget them in his effort to choke the nausea. The nausea was a familiar feeling, but for that reason its course was predictable. Above all he did not want

28

to be sick: it would be a greater humiliation than all the rest. As he left the messhall in the orderly file, his breath came more easily and his stomach muscles stopped twitching. The cold morning air helped more than anything. It was still dark and the fog was heavy in the air. For a moment before the company started trotting again away from the messhall, as he pumped the heavy cold air in his lungs, he felt sound and wholesome again; but when he started running, the nausea came on swiftly, rising. It was four hundred yards back to the barracks and it was too much for him. When the Sergeant called the halt, his throat opened, and he retched. He ducked back so that he would not soil the man ahead of him, and he fell to his knees, as if before a familiar toilet bowl in his own home. As he bent forward, Osgood took him by the shoulders and held him; even as his stomach turned, Gillespie was grateful, for the comfort of it and for the solicitude behind the gesture.

He retched twice, and with the great pressure gone, he felt better immediately: he felt so clean that he was not even embarrassed in his weakness. By this time, the company had broken up into the work details, but Osgood remained behind. Gillespie blew his nose, holding with the fingers of his right hand below the bridge of the nose. He caught the foul smell as he stood up. He turned around and saw Osgood standing watching him. In the relief and comfort he felt, he did not remember to resent Osgood as the agent of his troubles.

"Feel better?" Osgood asked.

Gillespie grunted and nodded his head. He turned again to blow his nose and saw Sgt. Cann standing about ten feet away. He was watching with a pained look, smelling the vomit. The smell was oppressive in the heavy air.

"That's a hell of a mess," the Sergeant said slowly. He kicked a wet clod of mud toward the spoil on the ground. "I want that mess off the ground before the Colonel comes around." The Sergeant paused and looked down at the ground. "And what's your name?" he asked.

Gillespie blew his nose deliberately before answering. "Gillespie," he said.

"Well, Gillespie, you go clean yourself and then clean up this mess." The Sergeant turned away shaking his head. "Jesus, it stinks," he muttered as he walked away.

Gillespie watched him go. He had narrow sharp shoulders that moved only slightly as he walked. His legs were a little bowed. Gillespie felt almost defiant as he faced up to his departing back; he remembered, with a little surprise at his daring, that he had blown his nose before he had given his name. He felt almost cocky as he stood there in the cold morning.

"The son of a bitch," he said very quietly, and turned back to Osgood. "The son of a bitch."

Osgood was still looking at the darkness across the square where the Seregant had gone. "I think so," he said. He looked at Gillespie. "You go on and clean yourself up. I'll clean this up."

"Don't you have a detail?" Gillespie asked sharply.

"Not right away. They haven't put my name on all the rosters yet. Go ahead." He seemed embarrassed. He paused a little and then went on. "Hell, it's my fault anyway. You let me clean this up."

Gillespie nodded his head. "All right," he said. "Thanks."

"And you better go before than Shannon comes out. You might say something wrong if you see him now."

Gillespie was pleased with this statement; he felt almost formidable in his injury: he felt as if he were armed in his indignation.

"I might at that," he said slowly. "That bastard makes trouble all the time."

He looked down at the ground he had spilled his breakfast on; and spat. He felt full of righteousness. For an instant, he felt invulnerable. He blew his nose again and cleared a part of the foul smell from his nostrils, and then started toward the barracks, hurrying a little as he remembered that he had a detail to make that morning. He slapped his belly and felt it solid and firm once more. He remembered that he had been assigned again to the detail for cleaning the Colonel's quarters. He felt a little better but he could not rid himself of the black memory of public humiliation.

At the door to the barracks, he turned to see what Osgood was doing: he stood where he had stood before, with his eyes on the ground, shuffling a crust of mud before his foot. As Gillespie turned away, Osgood kicked the crust of mud away from him and started for the corner of the barracks. He departed into the morning darkness as Gillespie watched.

CHAPTER FOUR

Gillespie found Johnson, the Colonel's Orderly, with two other men inside the barracks. Johnson seemed to know what had happened and he seemed patient.

"Go ahead and clean up," he said. "But hurry."

"All right," Gillespie answered. "I'll hurry."

He went back to the latrine and washed himself. In a brief inspection afterward, he could find no evidence that he had fouled his clothing; so that when he had gargled and cleaned his nose thoroughly, he was again presentable: only a smell was left, and he could do nothing about that. He went back to the detail feeling bruised but still jaunty.

On the way to the Colonel's house, trotting on the hard ground, some of his resentment came back; the appearance of the house itself bothered him; the brick walls with their windows were blank and empty. The house inside was bleak and clean. Gillespie resented the extensive cleaning this house received, a cleaning that surpassed the cleaning his own body received. He allowed his face to carry a sullen expression as he followed Johnson inside; he clamped his teeth tightly as he listened to Johnson's instructions.

"Well," Johnson began, "what we want to do is shine this place up." He bent down and touched the floor, nuzzling its polish with his fingers. "Mainly we want to shine this floor. The Colonel likes a shiny floor."

Despite his proud and general resentment, Gillespie nodded his head with the others, in consideration of this comment.

"And that means wax," Johnson went on. "It's downstairs in the cellar. Also we want to wax this woodwork. It hasn't been done since last week." He looked around him at the men. "And that's the job," he went on. "That's what we have to do."

All the men nodded their heads again.

"I get it," one of them said.

"Sure," Gillespie added. "We all get it."

"That's fine," Johnson said. "Let's go get the wax."

Gillespie spent all that morning waxing the floors and wood-work on the first floor of the Colonel's house. In spite of himself, he enjoyed the work a little, smelling the acrid clean smell of the wax, watching the wood take a glow under his cloth; but he could not disperse his resentment and anger. Thinking of the foolish-ness of this constant and enduring cleaning of the barren house, his anger grew and flourished. Now and then he remembered the obscenity on the wall and the investigation, and his fear of the investigation compounded his anger: he stroked the wood viciously, striking vaguely at the Colonel through the Colonel's house.

At ten o'clock, Johnson took him upstairs for a few minutes to show him the work for the afternoon: the Colonel's bedroom. At first, Gillespie was worried and anxious at being in the sleep-ing room of the commander of the whole post; but he got over it quickly by summoning his bitterness. He inspected the room rapidly for the interest it had: for mementoes of the Colonel. He looked at everything. The only object he could find that belonged personally to the Colonel was a large framed photograph, tinted, of the Colonel's family. It was framed in glass, fourteen inches high and ten inches wide. The photograph showed the Colonel's wife and two children. The wife appeared to be about forty-five years old, smiling into the camera; both boys wore the uniform of a military academy. The inscription ran across the page in a single line: To Father with love Annie and the boys. All the faces were blurred under the tinting.

Gillespie inspected the photograph carefully while Johnson was in the hall; the photograph irritated him. Until that time, Colonel Vopel had been primarily an object of hate; now he became a man with observable connections to an outside world. In the guardhouse, he was the subject of rumor and calumny: it was said, among other things, that he sometimes kept women in his quarters. The photograph denied the comforting rumor. Gillespie always liked the rumors and encouraged them, and for this reason the photograph troubled him. He became conscious, bitterly, of the undeniable fact that neither he nor any other prisoner was permitted a photograph of any sort. He turned quickly away from the photograph: with the smell of vomit still about him and poor prospects ahead of him, it was painful to look into that domesticity. He felt all alone, without any support, without any happy chances to look for in the future; and he hated the Colonel. He left the room feeling that he was being driven out and pursued by the picture.

At noon that day, Sgt. Cann told the company that the Colonel's inspection had been moderately successful: Colonel Vopel had found nothing severely wrong or filthy in the barracks; and Sgt. Cann was pleased with this success, but he did not show it. He said nothing whatever about the diagram on the wall, and Lt. Camber was not present at the formation; but after lunch Gillespie saw the first prisoners leave for their interrogation. Gillespie carried this worry with him to his work in the afternoon, and when Johnson came in five mintutes late to meet his detail, accompanied by Sgt. Cann, Gillespie was alarmed. He wondered if he had done his work improperly that morning. He felt better when Johnson beckoned to him and to the other waiting men; Johnson smiled upon them. "Come on over," Johnson said. When the three men reached him, Johnson turned to the Sergeant. "Here they are," he said, "but I need one more, Sergeant."

"Another man?" the Sergeant asked. "Isn't three enough?"

Johnson grinned at him. "It might be enough," he said, "if we had all the time we need. But the Colonel wants quick action. You know how the Colonel is when he wants action." Johnson nodded his head soberly. "The Colonel likes to see things jump."

"I know," the Sergeant said with a wave of his hand. "I know how it is." He looked around the room. "I think I can give you another man. There's a new man who hasn't got anything yet this afternoon." The Sergeant looked around the room. Osgood was standing in the door to the latrine, watching. The Sergeant waved to him. "You," he called. "Come over here."

Osgood nodded his head and started forward. The Sergeant watched him come; then he pointed to the orderly. "You'll go

34

with Johnson here," he said to Osgood, "with these other men. You're going to work in the Colonel's Quarters." Turning to Johnson, he said: "Is that all right, Johnson?"

"That's fine, Sergeant," Johnson answered. "Thanks very much."

The Sergeant waved a hand and turned away.

In the Colonel's house, Johnson assigned the men to their separate tasks. He assigned Gillespie and Osgood to the Colonel's room, and set the other two men to finishing the waxwork on the first floor. After watching the men on the first floor begin their work, Johnson turned to Gillespie and Osgood.

"There's something a little different this afternoon," he said. "The Colonel wants some wallpaper cleaned: all the wallpaper in his bedroom." Looking curiously at them, he said: "You all know how to clean wallpaper, don't you?" Neither of the men said anything. Johnson continued. "Anyway I'll be there. We're using sponges. You go on up there and I'll bring the sponges up right away."

Osgood followed Gillespie to the Colonel's room. While Osgood looked curiously about him, Gillespie went to the window. After a moment, Osgood came over and stood behind him.

"Not much of a view, is it?" he said.

Gillespie waited while he drew breath twice, and then he said, carefully: "It's a hell of a view. It's a lousy view."

Osgood laughed. "That's right," he said. "I don't like it either." He paused after he said this, as if he were waiting for Gillespie to continue. After a while he went on. "I can tell you now I'm sorry about this morning," he said. "It was a hell of a thing."

"It sure was," Gillespie said. He nodded his head and let his eye wander carelessly over the gray buildings outside in the winter light. He had a sure advantage: Osgood had made trouble for him, and under the system of the prison, he had no right because he had no authority. Gillespie allowed himself a feeling of resentment and contempt while he waited for Osgood to continue; he transferred his resentment for the moment from the prison hierarchy to his fellow prisoner.

"I didn't think it was that bad in here," Osgood said quietly. "I'm just learning how bad it is."

35

Gillespie heard Johnson coming up the stairs and he turned from the window and brushed past Osgood. "It's plenty bad," he said as he went by. "I'd have thought you would have figured that out on your first night."

Johnson came in bearing two big sponges and a bar of yellow soap. He was smiling like an industrious housewife.

"We can get started now," he said. "Here's the sponges and all." His smiling face and brisk happy voice wakened the two men out of their private irritations. Osgood looked up at him in mild astonishment, and watched him set the sponges carefully on a chair beside the bed. Johnson straightened and looked at Gillespie. "There's a bucket in the bathroom," Johnson said: "Fill it for me, will you?"

Gillespie brought the bucket back, filled with hot water; it was blue in the clean bucket. He set the bucket down in front of Johnson, and Johnson started without comment to shave the yellow soap into the water. He cut the soap with a pocketknife, and the soap split cleanly away from the broad blade. Johnson showed enjoyment of the simple task.

"All we got to do is stir this up for a while," he said. "This soap will clean anything."

"It better clean anything," Gillespie said. "It's a good thing the Colonel has hot water."

Johnson looked up. "That's right," he said. "The hot water makes the work a lot easier around here." He grinned a little. "The Colonel keeps a man jumping anyway." He sounded pleased that the Colonel held to a strict cleaning discipline; it increased his natural respect for the Colonel. In everything Johnson did in that house, he displayed his great respect and admiration for the Colonel. Watching, Gillespie felt like challenging this manifest belief with ridicule or humor; but he refrained because Johnson was a pleasant man who had done him no harm, and because he controlled an easy job.

When the soap had melted a little in the water in the bucket, Johnson filled and squeezed out a sponge. When the sponge stopped dripping, he applied it to the wall in a long vertical sweep.

36

"That's the way," he said. "You got to keep the sponge dry or the paper will come off."

Johnson cleaned three strokes of wall, and then Osgood offered to take the sponge. Johnson surrendered the sponge and stood back to watch. He nodded his head and smiled approvingly as he watched Osgood.

"That's fine," he said. "You boys'll be all right." Then he went downstairs. Gillespie and Osgood could hear him talking to the men below; they started working quietly, not talking. Osgood did not offer any more conversation, and Gillespie was still enjoying his resentment. He enjoyed it the more because it had some effect. Osgood, a fellow prisoner, could not be indifferent; and he felt the awkwardness of his position. Gillespie guessed that Osgood was still thinking as if he were a patient in a hospital, as if he needed no defenses. Gillespie had been a prisoner long enough to comprehend his imprisonment.

By the time they had exhausted the first bucket of water, Gillespie was ready to talk again. His resentment toward Osgood wore quickly in the small room. He began to think of the actual indignity done to his person that morning in the messhall. Osgood as the indirect agent had little to do with that: he gave no orders. It was the private of the guards, Shannon, the man with the blotch on his belt, who gave orders; and the tall Sergeant, and the company officer, and the hierarchy above them culminating at last in the Colonel whose walls he cleaned. Gillespie turned his attention toward them; he directed his resentment again in that direction. Looking heavily up at the framed photograph of the Colonel's family, he grunted and threw his sponge in the bucket.

"We need some more water," he said. "We need some more water to wash the Colonel's goddamn walls."

Osgood looked up. "I guess so," he said a little reluctantly. "We're not doing any good with this."

"I'll get it," Gillespie said. He stood up awkwardly, rocking until he found his balance. "But what the hell," he said. "Anyway we've got good sponges." He lifted his sponge from the bucket, squeezed it out, and tossed it in the air, catching it as it came down. "The Colonel has the best of everything," he added.

Osgood watched him curiously, and then he grinned also. "Sure he does," he said. "He has a good orderly."

Gillespie, seeing an opportunity to wipe out his earlier extravagances, said: "That's the way with Colonels: they all have good orderlies." He waited for a moment and then went on: "And sometimes that's all they have anywhere." He touched his head above the ear.

Osgood laughed, and Gillespie laughed with him; the tension between them eased out of the room: Gillespie felt free to attack the Colonel. He picked up the bucket and turned to look at the framed photograph. He lifted his free hand and pointed at the photograph.

"You can see it there," he said. "Look at that family; look at the kids in the fine uniforms with the belts." He laughed derisively and looked to Osgood for approbation. Osgood turned with him and looked the picture over; he inspected it carefully, as if he were searching for reasons to approve it.

"It seems like a good picture," he said. "I like the colors."

Gillespie was disappointed but he did not show it; he changed the direction of his attack. "If it is all right," he said, "even if it is all right, think about this: you don't have any pictures. You don't have a picture. Isn't that right?"

Osgood nodded his head slowly. "That's right," he said. "They took them away from me when I came here." He leaned back against the wall and looked up at Gillespie. "But I got myself in here. It was my own doing."

"I suppose you did," Gillespie said. "I suppose you got yourself in here just the way we all did. How long were you out when they caught you?"

"Thirty-six hours," Osgood answered reflectively. "That's right: thirty-six hours in Liverpool."

"That's just right," Gillespie said. "I was gone twenty-four in London. I had a twelve-hour pass before I got on the train for the front and the division again. And now I haven't even got a snapshot." He looked up at the big framed photograph: "I'd like to spit in her eye," he said. "Or in the Colonel's eye." He looked down to see Osgood's reaction: Osgood had not moved; he was looking up steadily.

"You could try it any time," Osgood said slyly. "The Colonel will probably come home this afternoon." He grinned silently up at Gillespie. "Nothing to it," he said.

Gillespie dropped his hand, uncertain as to what to do next; he was surprised. He looked rapidly from Osgood to the picture: the woman's paper smile poured out at him from the wall. He felt that Osgood had challenged him, but that he could find no way to meet the challenge; he felt ridiculous, as if he had been caught stealing buttons in a tencent store. He stepped toward the picture; the blank smiling faces beckoned him on. For a brief instant, he thought of spitting on the photograph, but he rejected the thought with a sudden loathing, and in his anger at himself and at his frustration, he swept his right hand awkwardly toward the picture in a gesture of irritation and futility; he was off balance, and the bucket in his left hand made him awkward: he fell forward so that his right hand brushed the picture from its place on the chest of drawers. The picture toppled slowly sideways and Gillespie lunged after it but he could not reach it; the picture turned once in the air and struck the bare floor on its face, with glass shattering each way free in bright pieces on the floor. Gillespie was stunned. After the crash, the room was suddenly incredibly silent; he felt his heart drumming and drumming in the silence.

It seemed to him that the whole house was quiet. He looked once, mutely, at Osgood, as if for inspiration, and then he bent to the floor and the broken picture. Panting, feeling his breath hot in his throat, he swept the fragments of glass together; down below, he heard footsteps moving toward the stairs, and then he heard Johnson's voice, calling as if from a great distance.

"Hey up there," the voice called. "What happened?"

Gillespie crouched back on his haunches; he gasped once and said: "Nothing!" He waited and cleared his throat, thinking only how he could keep Johnson below stairs. "It's nothing at all," he said. The bucket caught his eye, in the center of the room where

39

he had dropped it. "I dropped the bucket," he called. "That's what it was."

"All right then," Johnson called uncertainly. Then, in a surer voice: "Be careful of the floor."

Gillespie heard the footsteps move away again from the stairs. He looked at Osgood, who had not moved from his position leaning against the wall.

"Jesus," Gillespie said. "O my Jesus Christ."

He bent again to the broken picture; he lifted the frame from the floor and turned it over: the print had been cut, sliced neatly by glass so that the woman's head was separated from her body; the paper flared outward from the frame. He stood up and set the picture back on the chest of drawers, propping it on the hinged support; he tried to imagine that it was not damaged, and that it might pass for perfect if the cut were taped up, but he had no success: the picture was clearly ruined; the frame was knocked askew. When he saw the picture, damaged, on the chest, he bent again to the floor and started to collect the fragments of glass. He worked feverishly, once cutting the thumb of his right hand on a sharp edge. He snapped his forefinger against the thumb and looked around at Osgood.

"Christ," he said. "How about a little help here?"

Osgood bent his knees in a rapid smooth motion and pushed himself to his feet. "All right," he said. "But what's the hurry? It's only a picture."

Gillespie lifted a hand in a gesture of caution, unconsciously raising a finger to his lips. "Easy, easy," he said. "Keep it quiet. My God, only a picture!" He looked at Osgood. "They'll crucify me for that picture if they find out!"

Together they collected the fragments of glass. Gillespie went to the bathroom and took several sheets of toilet paper to wrap the glass in; he folded the broken glass into a tight knot in the soft paper, and then stood with it in his hand, looking at the frame and the print standing on the chest of drawers. He felt calmer with the floor free of fragments; he tried to think what he should do next. Osgood went over in front of him to examine the picture; after a few moments of careful scrutiny, he turned around.

"She's a goner," he said cheerfully. "You sure did bust her!" He laughed a little. "You looked funny as hell falling like that." He shook his head: "Funny as hell." His hard face brightened with his laughter.

Gillespie waited until Osgood had turned to him and was watching him; then he shook his head slowly, setting his lips neatly and firmly.

"No," he said. "It's not funny at all. There's nothing to laugh at; not even for you." He paused, watching Osgood's attention come to him. "You were in the room when it happened. They'll get you too. They'll get us both if we don't figure something out. You can bet the Colonel will figure it," he said bitterly. "He'll have it figured out, you can count on that: the son of a bitch." The words came out fat and emphatic. "The son of a bitch," Gillespie repeated. The profanity loosened the tight knot of worry that was forming in the region of his stomach. He repeated the words over in his head, feeling a little daring, but knowing that he was safe for the moment, cursing inaudibly in the small room. "You seem pretty sure," Osgood said then. "What do you think you can do about it?"

"I don't know what I can do about it," Gillespie said. "I just know something's got to be done."

"It doesn't seem like much," Osgood said. "Just a broken picture."

"It's enough," Gillespie said. "It's plenty."

"You could say it was an accident," Osgood said. "You could say you knocked it over while you were reaching past it to the wall. Why not say that?"

"Because it's the Colonel's picture! If he knew, he'd break our backs for it: he's the big man around here." Gillespie shook his head violently: "No. Nothing like that." He paused; he hefted the weight of the glass and paper in his hand: it made a compact and cohesive mass. "One thing," he said. "We could throw this glass out the window. I think it would hold together. We could

41

throw it out behind where nobody would notice it. That's one thing we could do."

"But that leaves you the picture still. You can't throw that out the window."

Gillespie slumped a little; his shoulders sagged toward his chest. "I guess not," he said. Then he stopped and looked suddenly around the room. "I don't know," he said. "I don't know about that. Why we could hide the goddamn picture; we could hide it right in this room: just so we get out of here. Just so we get out before anybody notices it's gone. Then we wait it out. If anybody asks us, we say the picture was all right when we left. Hell, I could tell them I looked close because I liked the picture and the Colonel's family!" He laughed, and smacked his thigh with his left hand. "Sure, sure," he went on. "That's fine. Nothing to it." He looked out the window. "They'd probably think the orderly did it and then hid the picture because he was afraid to lose his job. And we're out from under. Now how about that?" He looked to Osgood for approval again; he was genuinely pleased with his plan. He watched as Osgood turned and walked to the door; Osgood opened the door and stuck his head out for a moment to listen; then he turned around, closing the door behind him.

"I think you ought to report it as an accident," he said abruptly. He looked steadily at Gillespie as he spoke. "I think that's what you'd better do."

"But it won't work; I told you that. They'd crucify us both."

"That doesn't make any difference," Osgood said. "I think you ought to report it as an accident."

"Even when I've got this other way? Even then?"

"Even then," Osgood said. "Maybe more then."

"You're crazy," Gillespie said coldly. "You're crazy. You don't know this place; you just came here. You don't know what you're talking about."

"I know what I'm talking about," Osgood said. "You want to put it all off on the orderly. I can see that clear as anything."

"On somebody," Gillespie said. He permitted himself a slight smile. "There's got to be a goat somewhere for it."

42

"On the orderly then," Osgood said. "And what did he ever do to you?"

"On him because he's here: my God, who else?"

Osgood leaned on the door, closing it; the bolts slid home under his weight. He shook his head. "I don't think you ought to do it," he said. The fingers of his right hand opened and closed, moved from open fingers to closed fist. He was not a big man, but he did not look small: his body filled his clothes in a proper proportion. "I don't think you ought to do it," he repeated. "I don't think I ought to let you do it." He waited a moment and then he said: "I saw what happened."

Gillespie nodded his head and leaned forward. "And you could tell it: is that right too?"

"That's right. I could tell it." Osgood said it without flinching. "I think maybe I'll have to tell it."

Gillespie started to step forward and then he stopped, changing his mind. He was angry, and he was puzzled by Osgood's reaction. He rocked back on his heels.

"Then that ties it," he said quietly. "That winds it up." He turned around and looked at the picture; he touched the flap of paper that stuck out from the frame. He looked over his shoulder toward Osgood. "I want you to look at this picture," he said. "You'll see later what it can do when it gets some help." He turned around and faced Osgood. "I guess this morning wasn't enough," he said. "You want to nail me right this time don't you?"

Osgood snapped his mouth shut with a little gasp while Gillespie watched him; he dropped both hands to his sides. "No," he said. "That wasn't it at all."

"Of course not," Gillespie said. "It was an accident. You had nothing to do with it."

"I didn't say so," Osgood answered. "I didn't say that."

"I know what happened," Gillespie said. "I still feel it: all the while you sat there eating your breakfast." Gillespie rocked on his heels, watching Osgood. He grinned across the room. "Now you want to finish the job," he went on. "You've got a good start."

Osgood stepped suddenly forward, as if upon an uncontrollable

43

spring; he held both hands before him, clenched. His jaw was set. "I'll tell you something," he said as he reached the middle of the room. He stopped. "You're all wrong! You're wrong and I want you to know it!"

Gillespie stopped rocking; he set his feet solidly on the floor and lifted his hands cautiously. "Maybe so," he said. "You may be right. You're in a position to prove it."

"Is that all?" Osgood asked. "Is that all you've got?"

"That's not quite all," Gillespie answered. "You're from the First Division, aren't you?" he asked quickly. "I heard you say that the night they brought you in."

Osgood hesitated before answering. Then he said: "Yes. I'm from the First, and I'm proud of it."

"All right then," Gillespie said. "I'd like to ask you to do something for me. When this is all over, take my regards to the boys in the Eighteenth Regiment; you can tell them all about Tom Gillespie." He straightened a little, waiting for his effect.

"The Eighteenth Regiment? You mean you're from the Eighteenth?"

"That's what I mean; and since Sicily too. Tell them that."

Osgood shook his head and then looked across at Gillespie: "That's the truth?" he asked.

"That's the truth. I could tell you about that regiment for twenty years and never say the same thing twice." He looked over at Osgood. "I haven't changed my mind," he said. "I think I'll put the picture in the Colonel's chest of drawers. The glass goes out the window."

Osgood turned away and went to the door. He opened the door and blinked at the light coming from the hall window. Then he turned around. "All right," he said. "I made trouble for you this morning; we're from the same division: maybe I owe you something. Anyway it's not my business what you do: go ahead." He shook his head and tucked his hands in his pockets. "But you're wrong," he said. "You're all wrong."

Gillespie turned away, feeling his triumph; over his shoulder he answered: "I don't know anything about that. I have my own troubles." He walked to the window and looked out; the window

44

opened on the front of the house and street. He decided to throw the glass out of another window. Leaving the picture where it was, he stepped past Osgood into the corridor. He threw the glass out the window at the back of the hall; the bundle of paper and glass landed in a clump of bushes, out of sight. Gillespie turned away from the window still feeling like a winner. Everything looked easy to him; the terror he had felt was gone and in its place was a feeling of confidence that filled him to the remotest corners. He had not been so successful with anything since he had entered the prison; he also rejoiced because he had been given an opportunity to impose his will on another.

On his way back to the Colonel's bedroom, he calculated his next move: he favored the chest of drawers as a hiding place for the torn picture. He found Osgood where he had left him, standing by the door.

"Half done," Gillespie said cheerfully as he went by. "The glass is in a bush in the backyard." He stepped carefully past Osgood, as if he were a dancer in a ballroom. He felt skittish and frisky; he felt as if he had no more responsibilities than a colt in a meadow. He stepped up in front of the picture, looked at it carefully, and then picked it up. He bent down and opened the second drawer from the bottom; the drawer was filled with socks and underwear. The socks were rolled and the underwear was folded neatly. Gillespie dropped the picture on top of a stack of underwear and then stood up.

"I won't even hide it," he said. "Just drop it in there." He bent down and started to close the drawer; but seing the orderly rows and stacks of clothing brought home to him the implications of his action: meddling with the Colonel's belongings, he was meddling with the Colonel himself. Suddenly in the image of the wrathful Colonel, his confidence departed; it left him feeling a little sick. He shoved the drawer shut with his right foot and turned quickly away; the right leg was trembling. He went quickly to the center of the room and picked up the bucket.

"We still have to work," he said to Osgood in an uncertain voice. "We can't get away from that." He opened the door and went to the bathroom for more hot water. The Colonel's toothbrush, hanging neatly in a wooden rack, reminded him again of the picture lying face down in the drawer; he drew the water quickly and went back to the bedroom. He went silently to work and he worked as hard as he knew how. He concentrated on the wall before him, and now and then, forgetting the broken picture, he felt almost comfortable with his sponge and his hot water. He did not look at Osgood, who worked quietly at his side; he noticed only that Osgood stayed ahead of him without hurrying. The house after a while became quiet, with the men in it moving slowly and smoothly about their work. At three o'clock, Gillespie and Osgood had almost completed the last wall, and Gillespie leaned back to survey his work. He heard Johnson moving below, and then after a moment he heard the downstairs door open. He heard Johnson step quickly toward the door, and then he heard Johnson shout, in the army abbreviation: "Attention!"

Heavy large steps rocked into the house. Gillespie jumped to his feet and Osgood turned toward the door.

"Jesus," Gillespie muttered, "I'll bet it's the Colonel."

Osgood did not say anything. He picked up his sponge and turned to the wall; Gillespie followed him, listening to the voices below. Johnson was not talking now: it was another voice and the voice carried authority. He could pick out only an occasional word from the quiet murmur of sound; hearing steps moving through the house, he turned to Osgood.

"It's the Colonel," he whispered. "Making an inspection. O Jesus." His comfortable confidence fell apart inside him as he listened to the stately murmur of questions in the powerful soft voice. The prison and the prison's terrors walked into the house and his heart with the Colonel; he waited for the steps to mount the uncovered stairs. Five minutes later the steps started up the stairs, and the tramp of shoes on the stairs was accompanied by the respectful voice of Johnson, explaining and apologizing. Waiting in the room, Gillespie did not know what position to take for the Colonel's entrance. He looked to Osgood, but Osgood was busy with his wall, as if he heard nothing, as if he knew only the wall and no other thing. Gillespie stood uncertainly,

46

preparing his shoulders and legs for the position of attention he would shape himself in.

Johnson pushed the door open before the Colonel and the Colonel came in. Again Johnson shouted, too loud, so that his voice bounced from wall to wall in the small room: "Attention!"

Gillespie and Osgood straightened stiffly, with the sponges held awkwardly in their hands. Gillespie heard water dripping from his sponge, and he wondered if the Colonel would notice. It might show that he had been working devoutly, or it might show punishable slovenliness. He loosened his grip on the sponge and the dripping stopped. The Colonel walked into the center of the room, and stood, with his hands on his hips, looking at the walls. His gaze did not touch either Gillespie or Osgood; Johnson watched him, frightened a little by his silence. The Colonel was a short man, and he had a small hard belly that bulged below his blouse so that the belt on the blouse was above the meridian of his belly. He had a narrow face and a round red nose; the nose rotated through the room as the Colonel slowly turned his head. The Colonel looked at the three finished walls, and then he stopped rotation of his head. He was looking directly at the chest of drawers. Gillespie felt his left leg start jumping inside the trouserleg and he tried to stop it but the jumping continued. Gillespie, waching, saw the Colonel cock his head a little to the left, as if he were trying to catch some difficult odor. The motion was almost imperceptible, but the Colonel's presence filled the room: for almost a minute he was silent. When he spoke, his voice was soft.

"Johnson," he said. "What's that goddamn smell in here?"

The Colonel turned his head upward and around so that his gaze could take in Johnson; and Johnson was stunned: he could think of nothing to say to this accusation. The Colonel fastened his gaze upon Johnson's face. When Johnson did not answer, the Colonel cocked his head even farther back, and drew his eyebrows together. "Well, don't you smell it, Johnson?"

Johnson shook his head very slightly: "No, sir," he said. He looked unhappy.

"Well I smell it," the Colonel said. "And I don't like it." He

47

looked away from Johnson, down at the buckets. In one bucket, there were several slices of the yellow soap dissolving in the clear water. "What kind of soap have you been using in here, Johnson?" the Colonel asked.

Johnson brightened a little. "The regular kind," he said. "The same as always." The conscious bracing in Johnson's neck began to relax: he had answered a question successfully. The Colonel paused.

"I don't think it's the soap anyway," he said. "It smells rotten in here." He paused again and dropped his hands from his hips. He turned slowly on his widespread feet so that he faced Johnson with the whole force of his compact ugly body. His face was unreadable. "You know, Johnson," he said slowly, "This is the room I sleep in. I think you appreciate the fact that I can't sleep in this room when it smells like this."

"No, sir," Johnson answered.

"And I will not sleep in such a room. I want this room correctly and fully laid out at all times." The Colonel looked at his watch. "It is three o'clock now," he went on. "I shall return at the regular time this evening. When I return, I shall expect to find this sick smell gone and the room in order." He bent his head a little and squinted at Johnson, as if to make a point clear which had been hidden before. "Is that clear now, Johnson?" he went on. "You will stay here and see to it, Johnson."

The Colonel looked once more around the room. Then he swung about and marched out.

"Yes, sir!" Johnson called after the departing back. The Colonel continued down the stairs. Gillespie and Osgood stood absolutely still until they heard the door close downstairs behind the Colonel. Then they broke the position of attention. Gillespie noticed immediately that he was sweating. He felt the sweat trickling down from his armpits. He stamped his left foot on the floor to stop the shaking in his leg. His throat was very dry. He could not believe that the Colonel had been in the room without noticing that the picture was gone; he tried to interpret the Colonel's statements, and he tried to interpret and penetrate his memory of the Colonel's impassive face, but he had no luck with either. He felt sick, as he had felt sick in the messhall that morning. He looked at Johnson, who had turned to the door the Colonel had just passed through.

"Jesus," Johnson said. "Jesus!" He shook his head, and then he turned again into the room. "Do you men smell anything?" he asked. They both started to move, as if upon command, searching for the ugly smell. Osgood shook his head.

"I don't smell anything," he said.

Johnson looked at Gillespie.

"I don't either," Gillespie said.

Johnson was baffled. He lifted his right hand to his forehead and wiped the back of his hand across his forehead under the hairline. "I don't smell a goddamn thing," he said at last. Osgood laughed uncertainly at the expression and then looked at Gillespie, who started a laugh and then stopped as he saw Johnson looking around the room. For a moment, Gillespie feared that Johnson would discover the absence of the picture; but Johnson's gaze travelled in a distraught and unperceptive circle: he was smelling the air; he was not looking for anything.

"What happens now?" Gillespie asked.

Johnson shook his head. "I don't know," he said. "I just don't know. But you heard what the Colonel said."

At the mention of the Colonel, Gillespie suddenly felt the sweat that had formed on his forehead. He lifted his right hand, aping Johnson's gesture, to his forehead. In doing it, the sleeve of his shirt scraped against his chin; and as it passed, he caught the smell of vomit. "O Christ!" he said aloud. Osgood and Johnson looked quickly at him.

"What's the matter?" Osgood asked; Johnson waited for the answer.

Gillespie winced a little under their eyes. Simultaneously, he saw it all. He had not cleaned that sleeve properly. It had been touched with vomit in the morning, and he had failed to notice it. Only the Colonel, without knowing its source, had noticed it, and with it perhaps something else. Gillespie could not bring himself to answer to the smell, however; he put his right hand in the deep pocket of his trousers: the compendious pocket held his hand, his wrist, the offending sleeve. "Nothing," he said. "I was just think-ing what will happen when the Colonel comes back." He met Osgood's eyes without flinching. Johnson nodded his head.

"That's what we're all thinking about," he said. He turned his troubled eyes away. Gillespie started to think about ways of cleaning the sleeve; he decided quickly that it would be easy. Then Johnson stepped to the window.

"But this isn't doing anything," he said. He unlatched the windowlock, and opened the window. The cold winter wind opened into the room. Gillespie shivered.

"That's the right idea," he said. "Air the place out."

"And scrub the floor again," Johnson said. "We're going to have to hustle. Maybe we can get rid of whatever it is."

Osgood stepped toward the window, in front of Johnson.

"When will the Colonel be back?" he asked.

Johnson looked up at him. "That's the problem," he said. "It could be any time; the regular time could be any time."

Osgood nodded. "We might as well get started then," he said. Then they all started to work. Johnson began with a brush and hot water on the waxed and shining floor, and he worked hard, in a quiet frenzy, on his knees in the cold wind. At the first chance he got, Gillespie went to the bathroom after water and cleaned his sleeve; he felt honest as he cleaned the sleeve, as if he were doing a just and honorable thing. They finished neatly at five o'clock; Osgood applied the last stroke, with a wet rag on the closet wall. They left the room to dry and went outside into the hall.

"That's it then," Johnson said. "That's all we can do." He stood for a moment at the door, with his nose wiggling like a hound's, and then he beckoned to Gillespie. "You smell it," he said. "See if it smells different."

Without entering the room, Gillespie bent forward from the threshold. "It smells all right to me," he said. "It smells like soap."

Johnson looked appealingly at him. "You think it'll be all right, then?"

"If the Colonel likes soap it'll be all right," Gillespie answered.

50

Johnson nodded his head in a serious gesture. "It's soapy enough," he said. He bent once more into the room and then turned resolutely away. "That's all then. I think we've done all we could. I'll have to take you boys back to your barracks."

Outside in the cold air, Gillespie felt a tremendous relief; it felt to him like the end of school in the spring. He choked down all his apprehensions in his great relief. He was even glad to trot on the way back to the barracks. The cold smoky air, cold at first and then burning in his lungs, made him feel momentarily clean again. In the barracks, for the first time he welcomed the doors shutting behind him, as if they were shutting the Colonel out; he felt protected. He sat down in a corner, away from Osgood, and tried to think about the evening meal; he did not notice the flat caress of bare stone that passed through his clothes as if he were wearing no clothes at all.

CHAPTER FIVE

That night, Gillespie waited for something to happen. He watched the prisoners going and coming from the interrogations of Sgt. Cann and Lt. Camber, the men going out apprehensively and slowly behind the guard, and returning quickly and quietly to the room afterward. They went out two at a time. None of them talked about the interrogations after they returned. Each time the doorlocks clicked and opened, Gillespie turned in a twist of fear, waiting for his name to be called, and filling up on fear each time a guard entered without calling him. For a long time, he was afraid to ask questions; but finally he sought out Nicoletti, the little Italian who had been working with the broom in the morning, a bald little man who sometimes had information when others had none.

Gillespie had once helped Nicoletti unsnarl a knotted shoelace before a reveille formation, and Nicoletti had been grateful. He showed his gratitude occasionally beyond normal requirements by asking Gillespie for opinions on prison questions and prison rumors, and then listening attentively. Gillespie had always accepted this flattery with a mild pleasure. In his search, Gillespie went through the big room from group to group, looking for the bright and bobbing bald head, but he did not find Nicoletti in the main room; he found Nicoletti in the latrine, standing attentively before the urinal. Gillespie was pleased to find Nicoletti in this comparative privacy; he walked up beside Nicoletti and nudged his shoulder as he went by. "Nicoletti," he said. "Hey Nicoletti."

Nicoletti turned his head, with a quick uncertainty flaring in his eyes; he grinned a little when he saw Gillespie. "O," he said. "It's you." He turned his head quickly to look around the room; there was one other man in the latrine and he was leaving. He looked up attentively at Gillespie.

"How's it going, Nick?" Gillespie asked. The position was unfamiliar to him; usually it was Nicoletti who sought him out. Because he maintained a mild contempt for Nicoletti, he was uncomfortable and hesitant about asking questions.

"All right," Nicoletti said. "How's with you?"

Gillespie shrugged his shoulders. "Like always," he said. "I don't know what's going on here." He turned away from the urinal, and Nicoletti turned with him. Nicoletti looked once more about the room and then moved closer to Gillespie.

"There's something up," he said. "I'll tell you that." He put on a look of mystery, as if he were concealing dangerous knowledge. "You bet," he went on. "There's something up."

"You mean the picture on the wall?" Gillespie asked with a smile. "I know about that."

"That's it," Nicoletti said quickly. "That's what it is."

"That's nothing then," Gillespie said with relief. "That's nothing to me."

"You think it's nothing," Nicoletti said, a little resentfully. "But I heard some of the other guys talking." He looked up at Gillespie with wideopen brown eyes; the lids were retracted. Gillespie could see the eyeball, complete, in each eye. The face worked with the knowledge the mind contained. Nicoletti nodded his head gravely, three times. "Yeah," he said. "I heard some guys talking." He touched Gillespie's sleeve as if asking for more questions, but Gillespie pulled away; he felt a rise of confidence in watching Nicoletti, and in thinking that the profane picture was the only catastrophe working its way through the prison. For a moment, he wavered between letting Nicoletti go and holding him for his information. He felt that if he let him go, he could build his troubled vanity with a gesture; but he held him.

"Well," he said. "What did you hear?"

Nicoletti was pleased; he shuffled nearer and looked once more around the room. "All right," he said. "I heard the Colonel's been over here tonight to see the Lieutenant."

Gillespie felt a sudden shiver at the base of his neck; the shiver travelled down his back. He shook his head. "What was that again?" he asked.

Nicoletti was pleased with his effect. He nodded his head

again. "That's something new!" he said. "What do you think of that?"

"It's something," Gillespie agreed. "Did he come alone?"

Nicoletti shook his head. "I don't know," he said. "I didn't hear anything about that."

"Do you know why he came?"

Nicoletti looked up, a little surprised. "Why sure," he said. "I've already told you: the picture on the wall. Why else would he come over here?"

Gillespie nodded his head quickly in agreement, to forestall any questions that Nicoletti might put to him.

"Sure," he said. "That's it. I guess there will be real trouble now, with the Colonel interested."

"Maybe so," Nicoletti said. "He can put on the heat all right."

The door to the latrine opened and one of the prisoners walked in. Nicoletti turned away, and went to one of the washbowls.

"I got to wash up," he said over his shoulder. "Before they close this place up." He turned on a faucet and dipped his hands in the running water. Gillespie, seeing that Nicoletti wanted to stop talking, turned and went out of the latrine. He took his blanket from its place on the shelf, found a place near the wall, and spread the blanket on the floor. He wrapped himself carefully in the blanket and closed his eyes, but he found that he could not sleep; he could not even keep his eyes closed. He thought about the vengeful Colonel sweeping the room for him, venting his omnipotent wrath upon him; he felt like a proper target for that vengeance. He rolled slowly from side to side, wide awake, for three hours before he slept.

The next morning, Gillespie, Osgood, and the other two men who had been on the work detail in the Colonel's house the day before were called aside by Sgt. Cann after the reveille formation. All the men were frightened by this departure from custom and routine; Gillespie more than the others because he thought he knew what was going to happen. He was almost resigned to disaster; he centered his feeling of apprehension on what the Sergeant would say. When they came before the Sergeant, they stood

54

at attention, each man hoping that his flattery might help him. Osgood hesitated at first, but then he followed the example of the others. The Sergeant inspected each man with his flashlight, in accordance with his habit, before speaking.

"I suppose you men know why I called you out," he began. "At least you ought to know." He turned his flashlight on Osgood.

"Do you know?" he asked.

Osgood did not hesitate. "No," he said. "I don't know."

The Sergeant held the light steadily in his eyes. "You're sure you don't know?"

"I'm sure," Osgood answered.

The Sergeant dropped the light and stood without speaking for a moment. "Then I'll tell you," he said. He spoke directly at Osgood. "I called you out because you men are going on a special detail for the rest of the week." He waited and then he said: "Colonel Vopel ordered it. He said you men did a very poor job in cleaning his quarters." The Sergeant played his light quickly over the faces of all four men. "You men know what that makes us look like: it makes us look bad." The Sergeant drew himself up. "We don't like that kind of attention." He pointed the beam of light at Osgood. "Do you understand that?" he asked.

"I understand it," Osgood answered. He paused for a moment, as if he were choosing words for an important declaration. Then he said: "The Colonel put the heat on you: you're in trouble too."

The Sergeant's mouth snapped shut in a gesture of surprise. "I didn't ask for an opinion," he said savagely. "I asked for an answer, and that's all I asked for." He stepped forward one step and then stood straight with his feet separated widely. "Don't give me anything else. Don't get clever with me." The Sergeant looked suddenly down at the papers in his hand; then, with one finger marking a place, he said: "You're Osgood, aren't you?"

"That's right, Sergeant," Osgood answered mildly. "That's my name."

"I'm going to remember you, Osgood," the Sergeant continued. "You've given me two reasons already for remembering you." Then he turned the beam of light upon the other men. "And I want all of you to do the same," he said; the anger was still in his voice. "Watch what you say when you answer a question!"

The men stood rigidly at attention before him, all somewhat astonished at Osgood's small rebellion, and resentful because they feared the Sergeant would exact retribution for this offense from them all. Gillespie was further troubled because at this time more than ever, he wished to avoid all official attention; he wished to remain anonymous: a name and a number on a roster. The Sergeant waited for thirty seconds, in a rhetorical pause, before he continued. "This detail won't be pleasant at all," he said. "You're going to get all the dirty work we can find. It's a disciplinary matter, and we are going to treat it as a disciplinary matter. And you're going to work. If I hear of any loafing, I'll see that something is done to stop it, and stop it quick. Is that clear to all of you?"

The Sergeant watched the heads nodding; with his light he forced a reluctant nod from Osgood. He seemed satisfied with the response. "You'll fall out together after breakfast and wait for the morning guard," he concluded. "He'll have you for this detail. Now get on inside and start cleaning up the barracks."

The special detail started unpleasantly that morning. The task assigned was to clean up after a broken sewer pipe. The pipe, leading away from the toilets in one of the other barracks, had been exposed by a roadlevelling operation, and the blade of a bulldozer had split it open. The cut was vertical; it opened up five inches of pipe. The contents of the pipe had run for ten hours after the accident into the frozen mud of the roadside; the men on the detail worked for an hour and a half at cleaning it up, with shovels and one wheelbarrow. After that, until noon, they cleaned out by hand all the greasetraps in the kitchens of the big messhall. Of the four men, Gillespie worked the most diligently; he hoped that a good report would go back to the Sergeant about his efforts: he did not wish to miss any opportunity to establish his innocence by his industry.

He avoided Osgood because Osgood was an open rebel and because Osgood knew where the broken photograph lay. At the same time, with each passing hour, he wanted to talk about his troubles; he wanted reassurance, that his trick would be successful, that if it were not successful, he might still escape the punishment, or that the Colonel would not miss the broken picture. He cheered himself for a brief moment with these hopes. He knew that the only man he could talk to was Osgood; he was sure he could trust Osgood. By noontime, he was anxious to find an opportunity to talk to Osgood, but he had no chance until late in the afternoon, when they were working outside, clearing the ditch at the side of a newly surfaced road. This work was normally asigned to prisoners in good status, because the work was out in the open and honest; but the special detail, goaded sharply by the guard, found the work difficult and exhausting. They had only one rest period, at four-thirty, for ten minutes, and it was at this time that Gillespie approached Osgood. Remembering his last talk with Osgood, Gillespie was careful with his approach; he feared a rebuff. He waited until Osgood sat down, and then he sat down facing him, about three feet away. After looking toward the guard, and seeing the other two prisoners talking quietly, he leaned toward Osgood.

"It sure is cold," Gillespie said. "I'm freezing."

Osgood looked up at him for a moment and then looked down again at his shovel; he paused for a moment, and then he looked up again: "It's cold enough," he said. "But I like the fresh air."

Gillespie, eager, leaned forward, pushing a smile on before him. "Yes," he said. "That's one good thing about the job." He relaxed back into his previous position, pleased that he had made a successful entry; he sat without speaking, waiting for an opportunity to come to the point of his effort: his own troubles. He watched Osgood; Osgood sat at ease, resting well, with his shoulders slumped down around the shaft of his shovel. Gillespie watched the guard until the guard's back was turned and then he began again.

"That was pretty good this morning," he said softly. He waited until Osgood looked up. "You really told the Sergeant this morning," Gillespie went on. "You really told him." Gillespie nodded his head up and down in a gesture of approval, holding his face rigid in its grin, and thinking at the same time how he wished that Osgood had kept silent that morning. Osgood said nothing; he nodded his head a little, and Gillespie took it for a sign that Osgood was willing to listen. "I wonder why they put us on this detail?" Gillespie asked; and this time he waited for an answer. Osgood jerked his head up.

"There are plenty of reasons," he said. "I can think of plenty." Gillespie bent his head before the straight stare in Osgood's eyes, but he did not give up his intention.

"You think the Colonel found the picture?" Gillespie asked. He looked up again, hoping for anything that might encourage or aid him. Osgood looked at him with all the expression withdrawn from his eyes, as by a conscious effort; by a well measured restraint.

"I don't know about that," he said. "I know what they tell me; and they told me that we didn't clean the Colonel's quarters the way the Colonel wanted them cleaned."

Gillespie nodded his head in agreement, as if he missed the implications of what he had heard.

"That's what they told us," he said. "But I can't help wondering."

Osgood, listening with his head down, looked up with a grin tightening the corners of his mouth: "I'll bet you can't," he said. "I'll bet you're wondering. You've got all the reasons a man could ever need for wondering." Osgood slowly dropped his head, and paused. "But you no more than any of us," he said slowly. "We're all caught in it now." He shook his head, and then started to get up as the guard called them. He braced to his feet on the support of the shovel and turned to his work; he tipped his shovel against the frozen crust of the bare ground and drove it home with a hard kick of his right heel.

CHAPTER SIX

That night, at seven o'clock, Gillespie was called out for questioning about the drawing on the barracks wall. Shannon the guard called his name from outside the screen door, loudly, three times, and then waited impatiently, knocking once on the frame of the door to hurry him on his way. Gillespie hurried; after stumbling once and almost falling over the legs of a man wrapped in a blanket, he trotted quickly to the front of the big room. He followed Shannon with a swift attentiveness, as if he were going toward a meal or a cup of whiskey. He tried to forget his anxiety so that he could perfect his following motions; but Shannon did not once look around. Gillespie spilled his evidences of discipline upon an unheeding back; his good intentions were dissipated in the cold night air.

As they entered the narrow tarpaper building that served as an office building for the prison officials, Gillespie began to feel a little resentment as he remembered that Shannon had punished him in the messhall; he felt a little relief as he thought that in a moment Shannon woud have to deliver him to someone else.

Shannon took him inside the building, and instructed him to wait in the hall before a door. Shannon took a chair from the end of the hall, propped his rifle against a wall, and sat down. Watching Gillespie, he lit a cigarette; the smoke drifted in long lines through the close air of the hall.

"You wait there," Shannon said. "They'll call you in after while."

Gillespie stood awkwardly in the middle of the hall, looking from the door to the wall the door was set in; he did not look at Shannon. He guessed that Shannon was trying to worry him with the tobacco smoke; the smoke was acrid in the narrow hall. Gillespie was afraid that Shannon might play an unpleasant game with him in order to pass the time. He shifted his weight from foot to foot and listened to the voices coming from the room behind the door. He recognized the voice of Sgt. Cann, and now and then he heard of the voice of Lt. Camber. He heard an unfamiliar voice answering questions, but he could not hear all the words spoken; the voices were talking about charcoal.

He felt a strong relief when, after five minutes in the hall, the door opened and Sgt. Cann came out into the hall; Gillespie was relieved to escape Shannon for a time.

"You can take this one back," the Sergeant said. "We're done with him." He stepped back, and a prisoner, in the familiar green cottons, slid respectfully past him into the hall. Gillespie recognized his face but he did not look long at him. The Sergeant looked past Gillespie at Shannon, who was on his feet now.

"Who's this?" the Sergeant asked.

"His name's Gillespie," Shannon answered. "The next on the list."

The Sergeant waved a hand at Gillespie. "Come on in," the Sergeant said; and turned into the room.

Gillespie followed him. For a moment he was ready to salute the officer he knew he would find there; but he remembered in time that the privilege of saluting had been removed from him, and he held his right hand at his side. The room was small: it held a wooden desk, and two straightbacked chairs. Lt. Camber sat behind the desk, and Sgt. Cann was lowering himself into one of the chairs. Gillespie walked uncertainly into the room and stood hesitantly in front of the desk, under the open bulb in the ceiling that lighted the room; he felt the light along the upper rims of his eyeballs. Lt. Camber was looking at the upper sheet of a sheaf of papers on the desk. Gillespie, not wishing to show undue curiosity, did not look at the papers; he looked at the wall behind the Lieutenant, and at the door in the wall that opened into another interior room. There was a small woodstove in the corner of the room behind the desk, and its heat filled the room. Gillespie began to sweat.

When the Lieutenant looked up from the papers, Gillespie straightened tighter in his position of attention.

"Gillespie," the Lieutenant began. "You know why you're here.

We're investigating a drawing that appeared on a wall in your barracks. That drawing constitutes an offense. It is an offense in itself, and it is a breach of discipline." The Lieutenant paused for a moment as if he were remembering a memorized set speech. "In addition, that drawing has come to the attention of Colonel Vopel," he went on. "And Colonel Vopel wants us to find the prisoner who drew that picture. Is the situation clear to you, Gillespie?"

"Yes sir," Gillespie answered.

"Before I ask any questions, I'll tell you one more thing, as I've told all the men who have been questioned here: that I'm not forgetting that my name was attached to that drawing. Anyone who helps me find the man who made the drawing will be remembered. Do you see what I mean, Gillespie?"

Gillespie nodded his head to indicate a complete understanding. "Yes sir," he said.

"And I can be very harsh, too, Gillespie, on anyone who obstructs my investigation. And I will be harsh if I find that harshness is required."

"Yes sir," Gillespie said.

"All right then, Gillespie. Now where were you sleeping on the night the drawing was made? That was three nights ago, Monday night."

Gillespie was quick with his answer. "I was sleeping right near the door, sir. Near the inside door."

"Did anything wake you during the night, Gillespie?"

"No, sir. Only when the guard brought in a new man."

"And when was that?"

"I don't know exactly, sir. I guess about eleven o'clock."

The Lieutenant turned to Sgt. Cann. "Do you remember that, Sergeant?" he asked.

The Sergeant ran his hand through his hair and then he said: "I think so. We haven't had any since then."

The Lieutenant turned again to Gillespie. "Do you know who that new man was, Gillespie?"

"I think his name is Osgood," Gillespie said.

The Sergeant looked up from his chair; he had the chair tilted back. He looked up sleepily and then with interest. "You think his name is Osgood?" he said.

"I think so," Gillespie answered.

"You ought to know," the Sergeant said. "You've been with that man on details for two days now. Haven't you?"

Gillespie waited a moment before answering and then he tried to recall his mistake. "That's right," he said. "I forgot it." He nodded his head. "Yes, sir," he said. "His name is Osgood."

"That's it, Lieutenant," the Sergeant said. "I remember now. This man," he pointed at Gillespie, "and Osgood were on that detail that messed up the Colonel's quarters. Jesus," he added, looking at Gillespie, "you've got a hell of a memory!"

Gillespie felt the heat of the stove come strongly to him. He wavered a little on his feet, waiting; the reference to the Colonel's quarters terrified him. The Lieutenant watched him closely.

"That's odd," he said to the Sergeant. "You wouldn't think he'd forget a thing like that, would you?"

"I wouldn't think so," the Sergeant said.

"How about that, Gillespie?" the Lieutenant asked. "Why did you forget a thing like that?"

Gillespie shook his head. "I don't know, sir. I just forgot it."

"Did you have a reason for forgetting it, Gillespie?"

"No, sir. No, I had no reason. I just forgot it, that's all."

"You're sure of that, Gillespie?"

"Yes, sir. I'm sure."

"It didn't have anything to do with that drawing, did it?"

"No, sir. It just slipped my mind."

The Lieutenant waved his right hand above the desk, in irritation. "All right," he said. "You forgot it. Now did anything else wake you during the night?"

Gillespie, relieved, said quickly: "No, sir. There was nothing I noticed."

"Did you hear any sounds that were strange to you?"

"No, sir. After the new man came in, I went to sleep and I didn't hear anything."

"All right, Gillespie," the Lieutenant said. "Now." He paused, and leaned forward above the desk. "Did you draw that picture on the wall? Did you do it? Did you put up that obscenity?"

"Oh no sir!" Gillespie said. Feeling his complete innocence of this charge, he filled his voice with all the candor at his command. "No, sir. I didn't do it." He hesitated, while he decided whether he should say that he could not commit such a crime; he decided to say nothing. He stood straight, swaying a little in the heat of the small room.

"I'm asking you right out, Gillespie," the Lieutenant said. "Don't lie to me."

"I wouldn't lie to you, sir," Gillespie said.

"Then I'll ask you again: did you make that drawing?"

"No, sir," Gillespie said firmly.

The Lieutenant grunted and looked down at his papers again. He looked up as he heard a door opening outside in the hall. He waited as the sounds of footsteps came closer to his door.

"I suppose that's Shannon with the next one," he said. He gestured with his right hand at Gillespie. "That's all for now. Shannon will take you back to the barracks."

At the knock on the door, the Lieutenant called, "Come in."

There was a momentary pause, and then the door opened. Gillespie, turning from the Lieutenant's desk, stopped as the door opened: he saw, not Shannon, the guard, but Johnson, the Colonel's Orderly. He turned quickly away from the door, hiding his face; he saw Sgt. Cann rise from his chair. The Lieutenant was surprised, but he sat up as Johnson marched from the door to his desk. Johnson stepped up beside Gillespie.

"Private first class Johnson reporting, sir," he said. He saluted the Lieutenant and remained standing at attention. Gillespie, feeling in the way, stepped aside, shuttling awkwardly from foot to foot; he saw the Lieutenant's right hand touch the air near his forehead in a surprised return of the salute.

"I'm reporting at the order of Colonel Vopel," Johnson said. "For duty, sir."

Gillespie stood at an angle from Johnson but he could see him. The Lieutenant gestured toward an envelope which Johnson held in his hand.

"I don't understand," he said. "Colonel Vopel sent you?"

"Yes, sir," Johnson said. "Here's a note from Colonel Vopel."

He dropped the envelope on the desk, and snapped back into his position of attention. The Lieutenant picked up the envelope, looking at the typewritten name on the envelope, and then turned to Sgt. Cann.

"Sergeant," he said. "Take this man Gillespie out of the room, will you?"

The Sergeant stepped toward the door. "Come along," he said to Gillespie. He opened the door and went out. Gillespie followed him, passing behind Johnson, thankful that Johnson was dutiful in not turning his head to watch; as he left the room, he heard the Lieutenant say:

"You may stand at ease, Johnson."

Gillespie closed the door behind him, and looked toward the Sergeant, who was standing just beyond the door.

"You wait here," the Sergeant said. "Shannon will be here soon."

"All right, Sergeant," Gillespie said.

The Sergeant looked at him with a vague irritation, and then went back into the room. Gillespie, anxious to hear what was happening in the room, but afraid to listen at the door, moved down the hall away from the door; he hoped that when someone came out, his exemplary conduct would be clearly evident. He hoped that someone would notice that he had not eavesdropped; but his illusory feeling of virtue dissolved in a sense of disaster: he could not escape the presence of Johnson, and the question which formed itself around Johnson's presence. Away from the door, he could hear voices, but he could not identify the speakers. After a minute, he had almost persuaded himself that he should try to hear what was happening; but as he started toward the office door, Shannon entered the building with another prisoner. Gillespie stopped suddenly, and leaned toward the wall, as if he were only shifting his feet for comfort. Shannon came in behind the prisoner, closing the outside door behind him. He walked to the door, listened for a moment, and then looked toward Gillespie.

"What's up?" he said quietly. "What's going on in there?"

Gillespie stood away from the wall, with his heels together; he shook his head.

"I don't know," he said. "They've finished with me."

"Did you talk to the Lieutenant?" Shannon asked.

"Ever since you left," Gillespie answered. "He just sent me out."

"Do you know who's in there now?"

"I think it's Johnson, the Colonel's Orderly. He just got here."

"Johnson?" Shannon said. He turned away, a little bewildered. "I wonder what he's doing here," he said to himself; then he turned to the prisoner he had brought in. "You go up there with that other man," he said. "Wait up there." He turned again to the door, listened again, and then turned away toward the chair he had placed earlier. He leaned his rifle carefully against the wall and sat down, looking all the time at the closed door before him. He had not settled himself before the door opened; Sgt. Cann pushed his head out the door.

"Shannon," he called. "Come on in here."

"Do you want this next man?" Shannon asked uncertainly.

"Not yet," the Sergeant said. "Just you this time."

Shannon jumped from his chair; he took three steps before he remembered his rifle. With an embarrassed look on his face, he turned back; he caught up the rifle and hurried to the door. At the door, he paused, and tugged at his jacket, to fit it more neatly under his riflebelt. Then he moved slowly around the halfopen door and into the room.

The door to the office remained shut for almost twenty minutes; during that time, Gillespie stood uneasily, waiting, afraid to eavesdrop before a witness, afraid to talk to the other prisoner in a place so near to the center of the prison authority. After the heat of the office, he felt the coldness of the hall with an icy severity; but the sweat he had started did not stop running in the cold hall. He felt sweat greasing his clothes under his armpits and along the small of his back. Twice during the interval, his left leg began to shake; he almost welcomed the shaking as a diversion from his thoughts. He jerked his body into attention as he heard the office door opening; he expected the Sergeant with a fearful summons, but it was Shannon who stepped forth into the hall. He tried to comprehend the expression on Shannon's face, but he could find nothing there but a blank pleasantry. Shannon closed the office door with excessive care, as if he were locking a safe, and then he turned to Gillespie; with the door closed, he began to grin a little.

"Come on," he said, with a gesture to Gillespie. "We're going back to the barracks." His voice was loud as ever, but there was a hint of humor in his voice.

"Let's go," he said. He watched Gillespie march past him in the hall.

Gillespie could not comprehend what had happened; expecting disaster, he could not turn his thoughts into quieter channels: he was almost disappointed. At the outside door, he looked back at Shannon, but Shannon only smiled; he gave no reprimand. He was smiling without restraint, as if he were infinitely pleased; his red Irish face was genial and warm.

"Keep going," he said. "We don't want to freeze to death out here."

They walked quickly through the cold night to the barracks. Shannon opened the outside door quickly, and with a happy gesture swung it open before Gillespie.

"Here we are," he said.

At the screen door at the entrance to the big room, he set his key in the lock and paused. He turned to Gillespie, who was standing behind him. He looked at Gillespie, and then he looked past him at the high stone hall, and the heavy door. He shook his head, twice, as if in pity for the stone, and then he unlocked the door. As Gillespie stepped past him, he caught Gillespie's sleeve.

"Hold it," he said. "Don't go away." He shut the door behind Gillespie, but he kept his eyes on Gillespie, holding him with his eyes.

"Would you like to know something?" he asked. His mouth was open in a wide grin; he held up his free hand to prevent an answer. "You don't have to say anything," he said. "I'll tell you. It's the last time for me. The last time." He looked past Gillespie into the dark room. "What do you think of that?"

"I don't know," Gillespie said uncertainly. "I'm not sure I know what you mean."

Shannon's grin extended into laughter; the sound of it filled the room and echoed in the hall. "You don't have to know," Shannon said. "You just won't see me ever again!"

Gillespie smiled nervously, but said nothing; he was aware that some of the men in the room behind him were wakening: he heard sounds in the room behind him. He watched Shannon as Shannon bent forward over the lock; when the lock fell into place, Shannon stepped back.

"You can say goodbye for me," Shannon said. "I won't be here to do it." He turned swiftly and started for the door. He looked back once, to say: "So long, boy. I'll see you some other day." He slammed the outside door behind him. Gillespie, touching the screen door, felt the vibrations caused by the closing of the big door; his fingers took up the trembling, and he smacked his hands together to check the vibration. He stepped suddenly away from the door, trying to forget Shannon's departure, and everything that had happened that evening; but the whole time, in a single image, stayed in his mind, each detail vivid, each minute remembered. He found his blanket in its place on the shelf on the wall, and he lay down there at the wall, feeling that he was unable to go farther; he welcomed the shock of the cold stone floor, as he told himself that he was quivering from the cold, and not from any outside terror.

CHAPTER SEVEN

Gillespie worked the next day as if he carried a devil twisted over his shoulder; at every sound he heard, he turned as if to answer a question. He jumped when he heard a decisive or a quick step near him, and once he found himself sweating while he was standing in a cool corner. Twice during the day, he spoke to Osgood, hoping for comfort or consolation, but he could not bring himself to speak of anything beside the continuing cold weather and the prospects of snow. Each time, Osgood answered him quietly, with no inflection of emotion, as if with each word he said he wished to end the conversation.

Failing with Osgood, Gillespie tried to exhaust his fear with his body, in his work: he strained his arms to lift weights more quickly; he pumped his knees high when he ran in formation. But that night, he found that he was again unable to sleep. He had hoped that he would be asleep before anyone was called out to the interrogations, so that he could escape the anxiety of listening; but he was awake when Sgt. Cann came to the barracks at eight o'clock: the familiar voice startled him as it called out a name. Gillespie rolled quickly on his side to look through the darkness, but he could not see to the door. Listening, he was sure only that Sgt. Cann was alone.

Three times more during the night, Sgt. Cann called from the door; and the last name he called was Osgood. Gillespie sat up without thinking when he heard this name, as if to answer the call himself. The men near him turned in irritation, cursing, and he lay back quickly; he could hear Osgood moving through the darkness, stumbling over the sleeping bodies. When the door closed behind Sgt. Cann and Osgood, Gillespie closed his eyes, and tried to concentrate his attention on sleeping. He rolled his head slowly to relax the tension around his eyes; he tried for a few minutes to close off his head from his body by rubbing the back of his neck: but his eyes would not stay closed. They opened to the darkness and the vague planes of the inner walls, but he could not fix the walls in one position; the walls wavered and moved away from him. With each moment that passed, he felt grateful that no one had come for him.

He did not hear Osgood returning until the screen door closed; then he heard again the familiar sounds of a man crossing the obstructed room, and the louder sound of the outside door closing. He waited for Osgood or someone else to call his name, but he heard nothing. After a time, he felt his breath moving more easily; reprieved for a time, but prisoned on the cold floor, he finally slept.

The next day, Gillespie was unable to keep away from Osgood: he could not check the questions that filled and frightened his mind. Once during the morning he tried to speak to Osgood, but the guard stopped him. At noon he found his opportunity; he caught Osgood in the barracks, ten minutes before the noon formation, as Osgood was leaving the latrine. Without hesitation, he walked up to Osgood and stopped him with a gesture of his hand.

"What is it?" Osgood asked. He stood with his weight balanced on both feet, as if he could stand for an hour, or run for an hour, as he chose.

Gillespie stepped awkwardly away, pointing toward a corner of the room. Almost whispering, he said: "I just want to talk to you for a minute. We could go over there."

Osgood stepped toward the wall, and Gillespie followed, pleased that he did not have to take any further initiative. Osgood went all the way to the wall, and then turned. He leaned slowly against the wall, adjusting his back to the plane of the wall. He grinned a little at his position; but Gillespie knew he would not laugh.

"What can I do for you?" Osgood said. "I guess you have me cornered now."

"I want to ask you about last night," Gillespie said. "I want to know what happened last night when you went out with the Sergeant."

"They asked me some questions," Osgood answered quietly. "They asked about the picture on the wall; did you expect something else?"

Gillespie shook his head. "I don't know what to expect!" He shook his head again, more slowly, to indicate a part of his fear, and he allowed his voice to quiver as he spoke. "I just don't know what to expect any more."

"You sound like it," Osgood said. From his relaxed position against the wall he looked at Gillespie; his grin departed slowly, by imperceptible degrees, the curve of his mouth straightening into a narrow line in his face. "But I don't know what I can tell you; I don't see how I can help you."

"You could tell me if Johnson was over there last night," Gillespie said. "Was he there?"

Osgood nodded his head. "He was there," he said. "I saw him twice while I was there."

"But why was he there?"

"I don't know," Osgood answered. "I guess he's working over there now."

"I don't understand it," Gillespie said. "Johnson is the Colonel's orderly. What's he doing working over there?"

"He may have lost his job," Osgood said drily. "Did you ever think of that? Maybe he did something the Colonel didn't like and the Colonel fired him."

Gillespie shivered; he snapped his head toward Osgood, looking hard; a range of possibilities, the ends out of sight like the limits of mountains, appeared suddenly before his comprehension. He looked over his shoulder, instinctively, before he spoke; but no one was watching.

"Do you know something?" he asked. "You sound as if you know what's happened."

"I don't know a thing," Osgood said. "They don't tell me any more than they tell you."

"Then how do you know what the Colonel has done to Johnson?"

Osgood, with a shrug of his shoulders, bounced his body away from the wall. "Is that all you've got to say?" he asked angrily.

70

"Have you done something you want to drop on me now?" He turned to his right, away from the corner, and stepped away from Gillespie; but Gillespie stepped forward and blocked his way.

"No!" he said. "You've got me all wrong. Can't you see I'm scared? I just want to talk to you, that's all; I don't mean anything like you said."

Osgood turned away from him, as if he were ashamed to look into his face. "All right," he said reluctantly. "But don't say it like you said it before."

"I'm sorry about that," Gillespie said eagerly. "You know what's worrying me. You understand my position," he added.

"I know what's worrying you," Osgood said. "But I don't understand your position."

Gillespie, feeling sure now that Osgood would stay for a time, stepped away, considering what he had heard, wondering how Osgood would accept further revelations; he longed to speak openly as if to a confessor or to a friend. He felt like opening his humiliation to a sympathetic publicity, but he could not be sure of sympathy from Osgood. With sudden resolution, he said: "I don't understand what's been happening; nothing is going like I expected: I thought you might know something about what's happening. Do you see? That's what I wanted to talk about."

"We're talking about it now," Osgood said. "I've told you I don't know anything more than you do."

"But you saw Johnson; couldn't you tell whether he's here for good now? Or why he's here? My God, all I want is a little help." Gillespie turned away, as if to hide his deep feeling. As he turned, he looked at Osgood, and was satisfied to see in his face a baffled angry look of sympathy; Osgood shook his head violently, like a man shaking water out of his eyes after diving in deep water. As Gillespie watched, Osgood's face changed.

"I don't really know what you want," Osgood said. "I think maybe you want me to tell you to forget all about it, that it's nothing; to do your work and forget about it. Do you want something like that, Gillespie?"

"I don't know what I want," Gillespie said bitterly. "I guess I want news from the office. How do I know?"

"Well, I'll say one thing," Osgood said. "I'll say you have something to worry about. I don't know any more than you do, but I can feel something in the air. Christ!" he added angrily. "You know all about that; I don't need to tell you that."

"That's what I don't know!" Gillespie said. "What makes you think there's trouble in the air?"

Osgood's face stiffened: anger merged with contempt. He stepped toward Gillespie and caught the lapel of his cotton shirt. "All right," he said. "You asked for it; now I'll tell you." Dropping his hand from Gillespie's lapel, but holding him close with the angry attraction of his eyes, he continued, in a monotonous inflexible fury of speech. "In the first place, you broke the picture of the Colonel's family, and you know you can't get away with it. In the second place, you tried to put it off on Johnson; and you know you can't get away with that. And you've got me tangled in it all, but you don't know what you can get away with in that. You were afraid to own up when you broke the picture, and you're more afraid now. And you want me to tell you what to do!" Osgood stopped suddenly; as Gillespie listened, there was a moment of powerful silence after Osgood stopped speaking, before he heard again the talk of the other men in the room. "Would you like some more, Gillespie?" Osgood said. He forced the anger in his eyes like a blow against Gillespie; then he stepped back. "O you're a beauty, Gillespie," he said. "You're a real beauty." With his head high, snorting his breath like a horse through flared nostrils, Osgood pivoted to his right; he stepped out briskly. For a moment, Gillespie was dazed; then, abstractedly, as if against his will and better knowledge, he caught Osgood again, holding him with the strength of his fingers. He felt the fine hard tissue of muscle in Osgood's arm, that resisted him instinctively, as if it could endure no restraint.

"Just one moment," Gillespie said, passing his voice softly over the irony. "Maybe I know now what I should do." He tugged sharply at Osgood's sleeve, as the arm itself escaped his fingers. "Just let me tell you." He spoke quietly, with a shabby authority threading the words together. "It's not too late," Gillespie went

72

on. "I could go in right now and tell them all about it; if I went in now and told them, would that be the right thing to do?"

Gillespie did not notice the surprise that quickened in Osgood's face; he felt the sleeve stop pulling against his fingers, and that contented him. "I could go right in and tell them," Gillespie said. "I guess that would be all right, wouldn't it? They couldn't do any more than they've done already. It's like you said: it's just a picture. I believe you were right when you said that." Gillespie looked again at Osgood, for the first time looking directly at him, without fear or anger, as if he were buying from a merchant some simple thing: a hammer, a box of nails, something like a tool, designed for use. In subduing his will to the will of another, he felt no humiliation at all; for a brief moment, he felt a kind of rarefied and pleasant satisfaction. "What do you think about that, Osgood?" he asked simply.

Osgood turned slowly, with a blank uncomprehending cast in his face; the anger and contempt had left his face, leaving no traces, showing not even the possibility of these fierce attitudes. Gillespie, waiting, became impatient.

"What do you think?" he said again.

"That's a hard question too," Osgood said softly. "That's as hard a question as the other."

"But you started it all," Gillespie said with a quiet shrewdness. "You ought to answer my questions now if never before."

"But I don't know what to say," Osgood answered.

Gillespie began slowly to wake out of his withdrawn state of contemplation; as he looked at Osgood, the implications of what he had said began to come home to him. Now that he had secured approval with attention from Osgood, he felt less sure of himself; he began to hear more clearly the sounds of the other men in the room: their talk, the edgy, fearing, complaining voices; loud denunciation in a deep voice behind him.

"Say something then," Gillespie said. "Say something."

"It's up to you," Osgood said. "I can't tell you what's right; I'm in it too."

"But would it help? Do you think it would help?"

"It might help somebody else; I don't know what it would do for you."

Hearing this, Gillespie felt a familiar chill crawl across his neck; the skin on the back of his own person suffering the rack of an unidentifiable torture. He felt a deep swell of anger at Osgood for stimulating him to an impossible action.

"You said plenty before!" Gillespie said angrily. "You had plenty to say a minute ago."

"I know," Osgood said. "Sometimes I talk too much."

"Then answer an easy question: should I do it? Should I tell them about it?"

"I don't know what to say," Osgood answered. His voice sounded surprised, as if it had happened on something inexplicable and puzzling, which the mind behind it could not comprehend. "I don't think I can answer you any more," he went on. "You're out ahead of me now."

Gillespie felt more and more like his familiar self; his clear understanding of possibilities showed him the way. He began to understand how he had been led to his fearsome suggestion; he began to see consequences again, in an orderly and sensible arrangement; he could again see himself suffering for sins he could not believe he had committed.

"I see then," he said, not bothering to mask his sarcasm. He noticed that he felt better; a spirit of arrogance had returned to him after his momentary apostasy. Nodding his head to indicate his full comprehension, and full of a feeling of honesty and personal honor, he looked down on Osgood. "I guess that's enough," he said. "They'll call us out soon to lunch." He carefully placed his right hand in the pocket of his pants, balling the fist and rubbing it slowly and methodically against his thigh. "I think I'll go wash my hands," he said. He turned away from Osgood, noticing with pleasure the look of new bafflement that had fallen across the earlier look of approval. "I'll see you, Osgood," he said carefully. "Take it easy."

CHAPTER EIGHT

That afternoon, the special detail was split up into two groups: Gillespie went one way to clean latrines, and Osgood went another; but Gillespie did not forget Osgood. As Gillespie went about his work, he remembered with conscious horror the suggestion he had made at noon; he troubled himself trying to find his reasons for making the commitment. He feared that Osgood might be indiscreet; he remembered all the stories he had heard of savage punishments in the prison: he saw himself beaten and bloody, and he pleased his imagination briefly by seeing himself defy his tormentors, but he could not convince himself that the defiance would be worth the torment.

He tried to calculate means of telling Osgood that he had changed his mind; and though he was afraid to speak again directly to Osgood, he was more afraid of abandoning Osgood to his delusion. His active imagination showed him Osgood, in all innocence, giving him away, and this image troubled him: he wondered how he could react to an innocent man's deed. He thought for a time of sending a note, but he received this possibility as impractical: the note might be found. He knew he had no friends to trust with a message. His worry invaded his work, holding his hand, making him hesitant; and twice during the afternoon, the guard called him roughly back to his duty.

He carried his anxiety with him back to the barracks; he saw no solutions. Before dinner, he saw Osgood at the other end of the big room, but he turned away quickly and began to talk to a man near him: he feared that Osgood would interrupt him before he was prepared for an encounter. He stayed away from Osgood successfully through the meal, and for a time afterwards; he sought a corner near the screen door and concealed himself behind three men who were talking in a group. They were standing and they made a barrier. He stood for a moment, deciding whether to lie down in the corner in concealment or to find another place nearer the center of the room; but before he made up his mind, he saw Osgood moving toward him from the rear of the room: Osgood caught his eye before he could look away. Gillespie looked for an avenue of escape, but the room was too crowded; he could move only in one direction, along the wall, toward Osgood.

Gillespie, with his head down, watched Osgood approach; he saw Osgood's face set in repose for the night. Osgood stopped once along the wall to step over a man on the floor, and then he raised his hand in greeting.

"Evening," he said to Gillespie. He smiled pleasantly, and for a moment before he caught himself, Gillespie warmed to the smile; he felt his mouth shaping itself into an answering smile. Then he checked himself. He looked down at his shoes, twisting his head from side to side.

"How's it going," he heard Osgood say. The voice had a happy inflection he had never heard in it before. A sense of loss and desolation sickened him as he remembered his intention; he was amazed that friendship should be offered him. In a sudden vision, he saw how he might retain the happiness in Osgood's voice, and build with it a new realm of friendship; but the vision did not last. His sense of consequences stifled it. Gillespie did not look at Osgood; he heard Osgood move nearer to him. Then, decisively, Gillespie stepped from the wall; with two more steps, he was past Osgood, who turned with him in surprise. Gillespie continued on; he heard the confused sound of Osgood's shoes, turning on the floor.

"I never know how it's going," Gillespie said harshly over his shoulder. "All I have is trouble and bad advice."

When Gillespie lay down in his blanket that night, he was almost comfortable; he was confident as he waited for the rollcall to the interrogations. He felt a mild sense of anticipation while he waited, as if he had nothing to fear; but he heard no summons.

After the lights went out, the noise in the room fell into a declining murmur of voices and snores and heavy breathing, and as this sound sank lower, Gillespie's eyes closed of themselves: he wondered lazily whether the investigation had been abandoned, but he did not have the energy to pursue his thoughts to a conclusion. After a while he slept. He woke once when the man on his left turned against him, turning his weight suddenly, but after he pushed the man away, he slept again as peacefully as before.

He did not wake again until midnight; hearing a sudden loud stir of voices, he rolled in his blanket. The corner of the blanket which he had wrapped over his head fell away, and bright light from the bulbs in the ceiling assaulted his sight: his eyes snapped open, blinking, into the light. Without thinking, he sat up, confused for a moment as though it were morning; and then he heard his name called in a nervous loud voice. With his eyes shut against the light, he could not see the speaker, but the voice was familiar. The man next to him, sitting up also in his blanket, tapped him on the shoulder.

"It's you," the man said. "You're Gillespie, aren't you?"

Without answering, Gillespie looked up: at the screen door stood Johnson; a pistol in a leather holster hung from his belt; he stood bent forward and squinting into the brightly lighted room.

"Gillespie," he called again. "Goddamn it, Gillespie!"

Gillespie moved in his blanket, to the side, to no purpose; in a swivelling stare, he saw all the men in the room, sitting up or squatting, a few standing uncertainly, all blinking in the light: looking for him. He felt the same panic he had felt when he had stood up in the messhall. Suddenly he remembered that his name had been called; he kicked the blanket away from his knees and started to rise.

"Here," he called in a choked and startled voice. "Here I am." As he rose to his feet, he thought foolishly that perhaps he should hold up his hand, like a child in school who wishes to leave the room; his right hand switched at his side as he stood up. Leaving the blanket in a heap on the floor, he stumbled toward the door, as he saw Johnson turn to him.

"Gillespie?" the voice came sharply at him, as if from a great distance with an irresistible force.

77

"I'm coming," Gillespie said. He stepped successfully over two men, but he stumbled into another; he felt his foot sink into a soft thigh; he felt the eyes of all the men in the room move with him. Now and then, a face would rise to meet his gaze out of the multitude, but in these faces he saw only the eyes, wideawake, staring, calculating, curious without pity.

Johnson had the screen door open and he passed through the door and out into the corridor; in the open space, in the wind, he felt an impulse of freedom: he took three steps past the screen door and stopped. He listened without looking back to Johnson closing and locking the door.

When the door was shut, Johnson stepped stiffly by him to the outside door, and swung it open. "This way," he said. His voice was low, without inflection. "Let's go now."

Gillespie walked through the door, holding his head up in an instinctive gesture of innocence. Outside he turned to watch Johnson turn off the lights in the room, step through the door and set the big locks. He heard a click, and the light from a flashlight swept out ahead of him, paving a path of light along the ground before him.

"That way," Johnson said, gesturing with the light. "We're going to the office."

Without speaking, Gillespie moved down the electric path of light. He kept his eyes on the ground, but he could see only the light: his mind was dazzled with light. The bulbs in the ceiling of the big room fused with the light from the flashlight in a blinding illumination. Walking heavily, Gillespie could see only disaster in the appalling brightness.

At the door of the office building, Johnson set the light on the doorknob. "Open it, will you?" he said.

Gillespie listened to each word, playing each word over in his mind, as he stretched out his right hand to the door; he tried to detect anger or indignation in Johnson's voice, but he could find no meaning in the words but the simple meaning of command.

The hall was lighted with the one bulb which Gillespie remembered; moving decisively, Johnson passed him and walked to the door to Lt. Camber's office. Without hesitation, he knocked once and leaned to the door for his answer. Gillespie could hear a voice through the door; he saw Johnson nod his head and raise his hand to the doorknob: he saw these movements as if they were movements in a procession to solemn music. He saw, even in the dim light, the back of Johnson's hand circling the doorknob: it was clean and white; the veins marked it trimly. He heard the lock fall open with a sound like an explosion in the silence that surrounded him.

Johnson jerked his head toward the inside of the room. "Go on in," he said. "Lieutenant Camber wants to talk to you."

As Gillespie passed him, he thought he saw the traces of a smile on the familiar face, but he did not have time to look more closely before he was in the room: the scene was set as he remembered it. Lt. Camber was sitting behind the desk; Sgt. Cann in a chair tilted back against the wall; the door behind the Lieutenant's back was closed as it had been closed before.

Gillespie marched to the desk, and stopped with a snap in the position of attention. As he remembered the last time he had been in the room, he knew instantly that the room was colder than it had been the other time: the stove in the corner was going, but it did not heat the room so solidly as before. He held his eyes on a point on the door behind the Lieutenant's back, and waited for a question; but the only sound he heard was the hall-door closing behind him, and Johnson's steps, two; and then silence around. Feeling the silence, Gillespie chanced a look at the Lieutenant, without changing the position of his head, and he saw that the Lieutenant was watching him with a full steady stare; Gillespie lifted his eyes again to the safety of the point in the door. With three men watching him, he felt the room fill up with his guilt; he felt his guilt as he stood before the desk unable to speak. The Lieutenant's voice split open the heavy silence: "Gillespie," the Lieutenant said. "Look at me."

Gillespie slowly lowered his eyes; the memory of the scene in the Colonel's house blurred his sight: before his eyes touched the Lieutenant, he wondered desperately how they had discovered his deed. Pleas for mercy rose in him toward speech; he almost called out before the Lieutenant spoke again.

79

"I suppose you're wondering why we called you out in the middle of the night, Gillespie," the Lieutenant said.

Gillespie nodded his head, feeling the muscles in his neck move in obedience to another's will.

"There's a very simple reason, Gillespie," the Lieutenant went on. Gillespie's head was still moving as the Lieutenant spoke, and he had to make a special effort to stop it: his head was moving as if it had a power and will of its own apart from his own will.

"It all goes back to the last time you were here," the Lieutenant said. He spoke slowly as if his words carried vast and imponderable meanings. "Do you remember that time, Gillespie?"

"Yes, sir," Gillespie answered. His eyes, which before had blurred the room in front of him, opened wider and focussed sharply on Lt. Camber's face; he saw the face as a whole face and not as an organ of a fearful voice. A fierce and leaping hope set his heart to beating so that his chest shook with it and he heard the sound like another voice in the room. His fears withdrew as the Lieutenant went on.

"You were called out so that you could answer questions, Gillespie. The reason we called you, and not someone else, lies in something you said to me the last time you were here; rather in something you didn't say. Do you see what I'm getting at, Gillespie?"

"I'm not sure, sir," Gillespie answered slowly. "I don't quite know what it is, sir."

"The last time you were here, you told me that you had forgotten the name of a man who had worked with you all of that day: the name you forgot was Osgood." The Lieutenant stopped and looked at Gillespie, who nodded his head to show that he remembered. "All right then, Gillespie," the Lieutenant went on. "I won't ask you about that right now; I have two other questions." The Lieutenant picked up a pencil from the desk and balanced it on the back of his left hand. "First: did you draw the picture on the barracks wall?"

"No, sir," Gillespie answered automatically. "No, sir, I didn't do it."

"Second: did you see who did draw that picture?"

"No, sir," Gillespie said again, shaking his head. "I'm sorry, sir."

Without looking down, the Lieutenant tossed the pencil into the air and caught it in the palm of his hand as it came down.

"Very good then," the Lieutenant said briskly. "I didn't expect anything more at this time: I expect more later, however." He set the pencil down again on the desk and stood up; he turned his head toward Sgt. Cann, who had risen with him. "Coffee, Sergeant?" he asked.

"I could use some, sir," the Sergeant said. "I told the cooks to keep some for us."

"That's fine, Sergeant," the Lieutenant said. He snapped his head around, with a conscious precision, and faced Johnson. "We'll leave this man Gillespie to your ministrations for a while now," he said. "I think you understand what we're interested in knowing."

"I do, sir," Johnson answered. "When will you be back, sir?"

"We won't be long, Johnson. I don't intend to sleep again until this matter is resolved." The Lieutenant stepped around the desk, past Johnson to the door; at the door, he paused and turned around. "One more thing, Johnson," he said. "You must remember that prisoners in this company are not treated as you have been accustomed to treating Colonel Vopel: you're a guard now, Johnson. You have Shannon's place." Laughing quietly, to himself, the Lieutenant turned and went out the door; Sgt. Cann followed him out and closed the door behind him.

Gillespie stood in his stiff position, half-turned away from the desk. He knew that he had been reprieved again, but he was confused by the Lieutenant's actions, and he was disturbed by the maliciousness in the Lieutenant's instructions to Johnson: he stood steady, hoping that Johnson would see the compliment in his respectful stance. Behind him, he heard Johnson moving; he heard the scrape of a chair being moved.

"You can turn around this way," Johnson said.

Gillespie turned; Johnson was sitting in the chair that Sgt. Cann had left. All four legs of the chair were on the floor, and Johnson sat bolt upright in the chair, with his hands on his knees, looking up at Gillespie with a bright intensity; for thirty seconds he looked without speaking. Then, slowly, as if he were quoting from memory, he said: "I guess you make trouble wherever you go, don't you, Gillespie?" He held up his hand to prevent an answer. "You don't have to answer that. You'll have plenty of answers to make later; right now, I have orders to ask you about that drawing on the barracks wall."

Gillespie, commanded to be silent, stood firmly; for a moment, he felt that it was ridiculous for Johnson to question him; he looked closely at Johnson, hoping to find some trace of the politeness he had enjoyed on other occasions: he saw only bitterness, and a fear that could not be concealed, behind the bitterness. In the hope that gathered around his desperation, Gillespie nodded his head once, and spoke: "I understand about the drawing on the wall," he said boldly. "But I don't know why you said that about my making trouble." He stopped, as if he had spoken only because he had to speak, in the interests of truth and honor.

Johnson jumped indignantly to his feet. "Don't say that!" he said. "I don't have to listen to you!" His body quivered on the chair. "You know what I mean about trouble; you know just what I mean."

Gillespie's memory flashed up for him the scene in the Colonel's room after the picture had fallen to the floor, and the tight confident feeling he had while he was concealing the fragments; he had the same feeling as he watched Johnson: he felt that he could control the situation. He felt the womanish irritation in Johnson's voice as a weakness he could use. He shook his head slowly from side to side, allowing his eyes to hang in a loose bewilderment in his face.

"I don't," he said. "I don't know what you're talking about." Watching Johnson, he saw Johnson open his mouth as if to speak, and then close it again uncertainly. "I don't know what you want," Gillespie said, breaking his words as if upon a great emotion. "I'm just a guy in trouble, that's all. Can I help you, Johnson? I'd like to help you if I can."

Johnson's face grew red; he caught his upper lip between his teeth. Gillespie, watching, felt confidence rise in him; with his bold words he felt that he had won his contest. He waited for Johnson to speak; fresh denials were forming already in his mind.

"I don't see how you can say that," Johnson said at last. With a sudden resolution, he stepped toward Gillespie. "You broke the Colonel's picture!" he cried. "You broke it while you were working in his room. You did, didn't you?"

Thinking quickly, and with a clarity which he recognized, Gillespie decided against answering; with his head bent a little forward, he raised his eyebrows and blinked his eyes, knowing from past experience the pitiable appearance his face would carry. He shook his head slowly, with an infinite pity pleading in his eyes for justice.

"Answer me!" Johnson shouted. As the sound of his words came back to him, Johnson recoiled from Gillespie, as if in fear of his own severity. "Well, answer," he said again.

"But I don't know anything about that picture," Gillespie said. The innocence in his voice was so palpable that he almost laughed aloud at his own cleverness. "I really don't," he added in a clear, level voice. "You say it's been broken?"

"Yes, it's been broken; and it was you or the man with you that broke it. You can't lie to me about that."

"I'm not lying," Gillespie said. "Can't you see I'm not lying?"

Johnson advanced toward him, with anger and unwilling belief sweeping alternately across his face. "Then it was the other one did it?" he asked eagerly. "Was it the other one? Is that what you're saying?"

"I didn't say that," Gillespie answered with dignity. "I said I didn't know anything at all about that picture."

"You're lying," Johnson said. "You must be lying then." He looked at Gillespie's face, searched it, and then turned quickly away; he went to the chair and set one hand on the chairback.

"I'm not lying," Gillespie said to him. "I'd help you if I could, you know that. You always treated me right."

Johnson lifted his hand from the chair; the corners of his mouth were trembling. "That's right," he said. "I always treated all you men as if you weren't prisoners at all; I always gave you the breaks."

83

"And I remember it," Gillespie said. "You were always fair to me, Johnson." Gillespie, feeling that he had won his argument, separated his heels a little to ease his legs; he looked once around the room, feeling it as a comfortable small room, not any longer as a hall of justice and punishment.

"But I can't believe you," Johnson said slowly, not looking at Gillespie. "The picture was in the room when the Colonel left in the morning, and it was there when I made up the bed. That night, he found part of it stuffed away in a drawer in the dresser. I know I didn't break it, and you two were the only ones beside myself who were in the room; I know all that. Nothing can change that."

"That's too bad," Gillespie said compassionately. "That's a terrible thing."

"You don't know how bad it is," Johnson said sadly. With his last word, he stopped as he realized that he no longer commanded the conversation. He hesitated, looking down at his feet, while he made up his mind; then he said: "Can you say it again? That you didn't do it?"

"I didn't do it," Gillespie said. "I could say it all night."

"Then it was the other one!" Johnson said. "Did you see him do it, Gillespie?"

"I've said already that I didn't see anything. I'm sorry; I just don't know anything about it."

"I know, I know," Johnson said. "I know you can't say anything now: this other man is probably a friend. But he must have done it. If you didn't do it, he was the only one who could have done it."

Gillespie saw Johnson's face begin to set around a new look of resolution: the mouth stopped twitching; the cleanshaven cheeks showed white again over the cheekbones. Johnson stood facing Gillespie, but Gillespie was sure that Johnson did not see him.

"That must be it," Johnson said mumbling. "That son of a bitch!" Johnson looked up at Gillespie. "That son of a bitch!" Johnson said clearly. "I'll get him."

"But are you sure it couldn't have been someone else?" Gillespie asked. Johnson's curses sounded obscene to him as they came from the pale mild face; Gillespie began to see the consequences of his success: the image of Osgood's face, grim and sharp and angry at the eyes, appeared suddenly in his mind. Gillespie shuddered.

"You're sure nobody else could have gotten in? Were you there all day?"

"It doesn't make any difference," Johnson said flatly. "I wasn't there all day, but I know what happened." Johnson's gaze shifted to Gillespie's feet, and Gillespie uneasily brought his heels together again. Johnson turned suddenly to the chair and sat down. "But this isn't what we're here for," he said. "I'm supposed to be asking you questions, and about something else than this. I'm to find out about a drawing on a barracks wall. Do you know anything about that drawing, Gillespie?"

"I saw it the morning after it was made," Gillespie answered. "That's the only time I saw it. It's like I told the Lieutenant, I don't know anything about it."

"I heard what you said to the Lieutenant," Johnson said. "Christ! What does he want me to do?" He leaned forward in his chair. "I don't know anything about this work." He lifted both hands, palms up, in an appeal to Gillespie.

"Why are you over here then?" Gillespie asked. "Why did they send you over here if you don't know the work?"

"I've told you why," Johnson said angrily. "The Colonel sent me over here and he called Shannon out to take my place. And now I take Shannon's place here." Johnson laughed, showing his bitterness like a forbidden flag. "You see what it gets me, treating you men decently."

"But why would the Colonel do that?" Gillespie asked innocently. "You didn't break the picture."

"That's what I told him," Johnson said. He dropped his hands into his lap; he looked down at the delicate veins in his hands.

"Didn't he believe you?"

"How do I know? He didn't say. Do you know what he said, Gillespie? He said it was my responsibility since I was in charge of the detail; he said he was sorry to lose me, but he would do me the favor of sending me to this company to work as a guard."

"I don't understand that," Gillespie said. "It doesn't look like a favor to me."

"It's a favor all right," Johnson said. "Working here, I can even the score; do you see that? The Colonel didn't say that though. He only said he'd check with me later to see how I was making out; that's all he said. He isn't through with me yet, Gillespie, that's what it means."

"It's not fair," Gillespie said indignantly. He nodded his head to indicate his sympathy; he allowed his face to supplement his words with a look of understanding.

"And now I'm up all night, out in the cold, standing post," Johnson said quietly. "Tonight I'm lucky: I get to stay inside. That's what I get for being decent; that's my reward."

Gillespie watched him; the face was still set. Gillespie began to sense a change in Johnson that put Johnson beyond his reach; he sensed that he would not again be able to say anything to Johnson. His fears returned, replacing his confidence, but leaving an empty place that sucked his worries inward; his thoughts returned to Osgood. He tried to banish Osgood from his mind, but the persistent image of the angry face stayed with him.

"But you can forget it," Johnson said suddenly. "I want you to forget it, Gillespie. Do you understand that?"

"I won't say a word," Gillespie answered. "I understand your problem."

"If anyone asks you, I talked about the Lieutenant's picture all the time. You forget everything else I said, Gillespie, you can do that for me."

"I'll forget it like it had never been," Gillespie said. "You'll see."

"But don't think I'll forget," Johnson said. "I'm not forgetting anything." He nodded his head so that Gillespie felt he had been excluded from the gesture; he thought it was as if Johnson were agreeing with himself. "I'm learning," Johnson said. "Give me time and I'll know all I need to know."

CHAPTER NINE

It was a full hour before Lt. Camber and Sgt. Cann returned to the office. During that time, Johnson questioned Gillespie about the drawing on the wall; his questions covered the day before the drawing was found, the evening, the night, and the next morning. Without any great concern for his problem, and with no animosity toward Gillespie, he phrased his questions carefully and asked them in a dull quiet voice; but he held Gillespie in the position of attention. He stopped speaking quickly when he heard the step of Lt. Camber in the hall. He stood up from his chair and waited in front of the door; he stood at attention while the Lieutenant walked into the room. The Lieutenant went to his desk and sat down.

"Stand at ease, Johnson," he said. He picked up his pencil again and looked at Sgt. Cann, who had found his chair again. "Are we ready to start, Sergeant?" he asked.

"I'm ready," Sgt. Cann answered. "I'm prepared for anything." He turned his head and looked steadily at Gillespie's face; he settled his features into an expression of easy patience.

"All right then," the Lieutenant said. "We'll proceed. First, Johnson: did you learn anything, Johnson?"

"No, sir," Johnson answered. "Apparently this man doesn't know anything about the drawing; at any rate, he won't talk about it."

"I see," the Lieutenant answered. He turned from Johnson to Gillespie. "You're exhausting my patience, Gillespie," he said. "You're being very difficult. I feel that I've already gone very far in leniency toward you; I feel that you don't appreciate my consideration." The Lieutenant looked down at his pencil, turning it in his hands so that the engraved trademark caught the light. He shook his head twice and looked up again at Gillespie. "Perhaps I should remind you of a few facts which you may have forgotten;

I might stimulate your imagination, if not your memory. First of all, you slept at the door, the night the drawing was made. Secondly, you are known to have been awake during the night. Thirdly, at your first interrogation, you lied to me; and it has been my experience that one lie commonly conceals another lie. Finally, we know you to be a troublemaker. You have been punished publicly for breaking a prison rule; you have been sent on a punitive detail on the order of Colonel Vopel himself, for having improperly performed your duties while cleaning his quarters. Can you object to my facts, Gillespie?"

Gillespie felt his face redden; he started a complete denial, but his intention dissolved in his better judgment and in his fear of the Lieutenant.

"I—no, sir," he said. "I guess your facts are all right."

"But you object to my conclusions. That's not at all complimentary, Gillespie. I rather pride myself on my powers of judgment."

"That's not what I meant, sir."

"You needn't explain it, Gillespie," the Lieutenant answered. "Your meaning is clear enough. Johnson," the Lieutenant said sharply, "just what was your procedure with this man?"

"Why I asked questions, sir," Johnson answered.

"Do you think you covered the ground thoroughly, Johnson?"

"I think so, sir."

"But you learned nothing. Perhaps you employed the wrong technique. Is that possible, Johnson?"

"Yes, sir. I suppose it's possible."

"Then perhaps you should try something else, Johnson. I suggest you go into the next room and try something else."

"Yes, sir," Johnson answered.

"Back here," the Lieutenant said, gesturing over his shoulder at the door behind him. "You can close the door behind you if you wish."

Johnson nodded his head and stepped toward the door. "Come on," he said to Gillespie. Johnson opened the door and went into the room beyond; when Gillespie had passed the door, Johnson closed it, setting the catches softly into place. Then he turned to face Gillespie; a look of determination replaced the anxious humiliation that had showed in his face. He shook his head slowly, as if to indicate his reluctance.

"Gillespie," he said. "You could save me a lot of trouble if you told me now. Will you tell me somthing now?"

"I can't tell you anything," Gillespie answered. "I've told you the truth about everything."

Johnson looked down, nodding his head. "That may be," he said. He stepped closer to Gillespie and whispered: "But what can I do? You heard what the Lieutenant said."

Gillespie, afraid to speak, nodded his head. Though the door was closed, he could feel Lt. Camber's presence in the next room: as if in answer to his thought, he heard a loud knocking on the door.

"Johnson!" the Lieutenant's voice said. "Speak loud enough so I can hear you!"

Johnson automatically stood straighter. "Yes, sir!" he called. He turned to Gillespie. "Go over to the wall!" he said. He pointed to his left: "Over there."

Gillespie followed the outstretched hand. He stopped three feet from the wall and looked back; a specific and localized fear began to possess him: Johnson no longer resembled a dupe or a friend.

"Put your feet to the wall," Johnson said. "But keep the heels together. Now bend down." He stepped up beside Gillespie and touched a point on the wall three feet above the floor. "Touch your nose to the wall right there."

Gillespie, following instructions, bent down; he felt naked. The muscles in his back grew taut. He found that he could not touch the wall without turning his head, and when he turned his head, his neck was bent so that he felt an immediate stitch of pain.

"That's right," Johnson said. "Now keep your legs straight." Johnson stepped back, out of Gillespie's sight. Gillespie could hear Johnson's quick harsh breathing. "Now then," Johnson said in a loud voice. "Did you make the drawing on the wall?"

Gillespie, hearing the strained loudness in Johnson's voice, guessed that Johnson was talking for the Lieutenant in the next room. "I didn't do it," he said.

"Did you see who did make that drawing?"

"I didn't see anything," Gillespie answered. His left leg was beginning to quiver; the knee ached as it had ached when he had been punished in the messhall: the stories he had heard of prison punishments changed in his mind to sharp images. He closed his eyes against a vision of his own face, but the image remained; the eyes were rolling wild. He waited for Johnson's next question.

"Then stand for a while," Johnson said.

The voice sounded incredibly controlled; Gillespie could not recognize its intonation. The voice sounded remote and distant. Gillespie waited for a blow; a sense of vast injustice wracked him. He became conscious of the cold flatness of the wood his nose touched.

Johnson did not speak again for five minutes. When he spoke, his voice was as loud as before.

"You can stand up now," he said

Gillespie arched his back quickly, but stopped his movement as a sharp and licking pain ran the length of his left leg. He turned away from the wall, bracing himself with his right hand against the wall. He straightened slowly; his body did not respond as he expected it to respond, and he was forced to prop every motion against the wall. He was astonished at his own weakness.

"Did you make the drawing on the wall?" Johnson asked.

Gillespie was amazed at the question; he felt it as an indignity after his feat of physical endurance. "No!" he said. His breath rushed from him as he spoke and he gasped quickly to fill his lungs.

"Did you see who did make that drawing?"

Gillespie shook his head. "No!" he said, in a long respiratory cry. "I didn't see anything." He looked at Johnson; Johnson looked down at him, twisting his mouth in a gesture of pity: he shook his head and shrugged his shoulders. Without making a noise, and without changing his expression, he mouthed the words: "I have to do it." He pointed at the door. Then, in the

90

familiar loud voice, he said: "Take the position again; just like you were before." As Gillespie turned again to the wall, he noticed a new look on Johnson's face: it was compounded equally of curiosity and a partially concealed satisfaction. As Gillespie bent to the wall, his body went through the same cycle. of pain as when he had risen; when his nose touched the wall, he closed his eyes. Then, for ten minutes, he wracked his body on the impossible angle. He became dizzy. Only his fear of more painful punishments held him; after twelve minutes, he stopped trying to control his dizziness. He felt vast reeling motions in his head; a red glow swirled in his darkness and he felt himself swaying: at a great distance he heard steps moving toward him as he fell. He tumbled stiffly backward to the floor; his buttocks hit the floor and then his body opened out of its angle: the back of his head bounced on the floor, twice, and then settled to the wood. With the blow, his eyes opened; the vertigo was gone, but a harsh pain invaded his body from head to foot, as he shivered in a fierce relaxation. He closed his eyes and then opened them again when he felt someone touch him: Johnson was bending over him, touching his shoulder.

"Are you hurt?" Johnson asked. "I tried to catch you but you were too quick for me."

Gillespie sat up and touched the back of his head. He was confused; for a moment, he did not remember where he was. He looked up at Johnson and saw only a mild curiosity drawn across the white face.

"O I'm all right," Gillespie said. Suddenly embarrassed, he started to get up. When he reached his feet, he turned around and looked at the door: there were two knocks on the door and then Lt. Camber walked in. The Lieutenant stood for a moment, looking, and then grinned a little.

"What happened, Johnson?" he asked. "What caused all the noise?"

"This man fell," Johnson said diffidently. "I had him lined up against the wall and he fell backward and hit his head."

The Lieutenant nodded without speaking. He glanced at Gillespie, taking in the bewilderment and the embarrassment, and then he looked at Johnson; he extended the nodding of his head to his hips, bowing a little: he smiled his approbation.

"Well," he said. "I'm surprised, Johnson; perhaps you're learning your duties now."

"I'm learning, sir," Johnson said. "I think I see my duty, sir."

"That's very good, Johnson. Do we know anything more now?"

"Nothing new, sir. It's very difficult."

"Yes," the Lieutenant said. "I understand the difficulty." He lifted his right hand above his shoulder to look at his watch. "Almost two o'clock," he said. "I think it's time to try something else. I think perhaps it would be a good thing now to bring in the other man; his name is Osgood. We'll bring these two together and see what happens. You know where to find Osgood, I presume."

"Yes, sir. I'll be able to find him."

"We'll wait for you. Meanwhile," the Lieutenant turned to Gillespie, "I'll try my luck with this one. Come on," he said to Gillespie. "Back to the office." The Lieutenant turned swiftly, with the precision of good health and confidence, and stepped through the door. With no feeling other than embarrassment and fragmentary pain, Gillespie followed. He was dazed; he could not comprehend Johnson's actions: he expected sympathy and a hand on the shoulder to guide him. He wavered in his stride as he went through the door, and he had to steer himself by hand away from the door frame. With a blind remembrance of the established convention, he moved to his position in front of the Lieutenant's desk. As he turned to face the desk, he saw Johnson go out into the hall: sudden realization pierced the dullness of his exhaustion. He thought of Osgood, angry always; soon to be wakened out of his sound sleep. He turned his head wildly away from the door, as if by the gesture to escape his entrapment. As he looked down at the Lieutenant, a vast confusion muffled his sharpness; he felt as if a nightmare had invaded all his intelligence, dissipating his power of planning with his power of standing erect. He blinked his eyes twice, to bring the Lieutenant's face into focus.

"How are you feeling, Gillespie?" the Lieutenant asked.

"I'm dizzy," Gillespie said suddenly. He shifted his feet and shook his head. "I can't see too well."

92

"It's time enough," Sgt. Cann said from behind him. "Maybe you'll shake a little now."

Before Gillespie could turn to look at the Sergenat, the Lieutenant spoke again. "Perhaps you understand now that we're serious, Gillespie. Of course, we do regret your dizziness, though we don't understand its cause. Can you tell us about the picture on the wall now?"

"But I don't know anything," Gillespie said obstinately. He was astonished at the shakiness in his voice; feeling that the shakiness constituted an admission, he spoke again: "I don't know anything at all. How can I talk if I don't know anything?"

"You're very stubborn," the Lieutenant said. "I really can't understand it. Perhaps I should put the matter another way: we want you to know something; we want the knowledge to appear. It is our hope that before the night is over, you will know something; and, further, that knowing you will be willing to communicate your knowledge. I suppose you don't understand that, Gillespie?"

Gillespie shook his head, feeling his confusion grow within him: it twisted his thoughts into an impossible puzzle. Nothing came straight for him: he heard a voice asking questions, but the meaning in the words escaped him; only the meaning of entrapment was clear in his mind. He pictured Osgood walking sullenly through the darkness, following the electric path of light which he himself had followed earlier. He did not answer the Lieutenant's question; nodding his head, he tried to picture his own confusion.

"I didn't think you would understand," the Lieutenant went on. "Perhaps you'll understand better when your friend Osgood arrives. We'll just wait comfortably until he gets here."

It was five minutes before Johnson returned with Osgood. Gillespie, thinking back over what the Lieutenant had said, tried to find the meanings which had slipped by him; but this thoughts were interrupted as soon as they started by the image of Osgood's face. Gillespie almost forgot the Lieutenant as he thought of Osgood: he pictured the wrath of Osgood, shaking the room, shattering his plans and all his strategies. He felt that nothing was going well; he felt his plans breaking up under the impact of their own success. He shuddered when he thought of Johnson and Osgood alone in the room behind the office. He looked down at the Lieutenant, and he was amazed that the Lieutenant could be so calm while such disasters were shaping themselves toward their climax in the night. He jumped when he heard steps in the hall; and he did not even try to conceal his emotion, although he felt the Lieutenant's eyes on him. He wanted desperately to look around when he heard the hall door open, but he restrained himself.

"In there," he heard Johnson say. "Go right in the door."

Gillespie could recognize only a part of Johnson's voice: anger had mastered the soft inflection that had been there before; Gillespie recognized only the high waspishness of the voice itself.

"You can stand up next to Gillespie," Johnson said. "The Lieutenant wants to talk to you both."

The Lieutenant looked past Gillespie at Osgood moving across the room; when Osgood stood beside Gillespie, he spoke. "I do indeed want to talk to you both," he said. "So that you will understand what I'm getting at, I'll go over it briefly for you, Osgood. Gillespie has heard it already, and therefore I'll be brief; and it is simple. You see, Osgood, we think that you and Gillespie know something about the drawing, the obscene drawing, which appeared on the barracks wall last week. We caught Gillespie in a lie which involved you, and that was our tip. We have brought you two over here in order to secure admissions of what we know; and that's the problem. Now, what do you know, Osgood?"

"Nothing," Osgood answered sharply. "I don't even know what kind of lie Gillespie has told you." He looked straight ahead of him, fixing the Lieutenant with his steady stare.

The Lieutenant looked up quickly, in surprise; then he turned to Sgt. Cann: "You were right, Sergeant," he said. "I think he'll be difficult too."

"I know him all right," Sgt. Cann said. "He's a troublemaker who always has an answer."

"Yes," the Lieutenant said. "You told me about that. It happened more than once, as I recall: do you remember, Osgood?"

Osgood looked down at the Lieutenant, pausing before he answered. Gillespie, seeing the Lieutenant's eyes on Osgood, turned his head a little to his left to look at Osgood: the face had the familiar stiffness, but a stiffness afflicted now with a dark bitterness. Gillespie turned away as Osgood answered.

"I think I remember," Osgood said. "It doesn't trouble me."

The Lieutenant suddenly angry, stood up behind the desk. "Shut up!" he said. "Answer the question; don't do anything more! Sergeant!" the Lieutenant called. "I want you to witness this." The Lieutenant looked across the room at Sgt. Cann, who had risen from his chair. "It's something we'll want to remember, Sergeant," the Lieutenant added. He sat back in his chair, picking up the pencil again as he settled himself.

"Now then, Osgood," the Lieutenant continued in a calmer voice. "I'll ask the question again. Do you know anything about that drawing?"

"No, sir," Osgood answered quietly. "I've told you once. I'm tired of pictures now; I don't want to know anything about any of them."

Gillespie jumped in place, dancing with the fear that took possession of him; he heard Johnson move his feet behind him, and he thought he heard Johnson draw breath quickly; but the Lieutenant's voice interrupted the sound.

"I can see that," the Lieutenant said. "But again: we don't want any comments. Is that all you've got to say?"

"I can't say anything more, sir," Osgood answered.

"Very well then," the Lieutenant said crisply. "I've given you your chance; now we'll try something else. Johnson!"

"Yes, sir," Johnson said, stepping forward to the side of the desk.

"Johnson," the Lieutenant said, "I want you to place this man Osgood for us. Place him in this room; I want to watch what happens. You can use this wall on my right." The Lieutenant gestured with the pencil.

"Yes, sir," Johnson answered. He touched his right hand to the holster that hung at his belt, and juggled it across his hip. "Over there," he said to Osgood. "You heard the Lieutenant." He followed Osgood to the wall. "Now stand at attention against the

wall; put your toes against the wall: that's right." Johnson took a
deep breath; he stood leaning forward: his right hand moved to
the top of the holster. "Now bend down." Johnson stepped forward and touched the wall. "Now touch your nose to this point
on the wall; and hold it there; and keep your knees stiff." Johnson
watched Osgood move as he had directed, and then he turned to
face the Lieutenant. "Is that all right, sir?"

"That's quite satisfactory, Johnson. Shannon himself could not
have done it better." The Lieutenant inspected Osgood; then,
showing his power in his slow gesture, he turned to Gillespie.
"You'll watch, Gillespie," he said. "You will observe that we have
not touched this man; you remember that no one touched you ex-
cept to help you to your feet."

Gillespie turned his head: the awkward bowed stance of
Osgood's twisted body caused a sudden pain in his own left
shoulder as he remembered his own position. He was astonished
to see Osgood obey the commands; he was shocked at the ugly
controlled fury that could bend Osgood's proud body.

"Turn all the way around, Gillespie," the Lieutenant said.

Gillespie shuffled his feet and turned; each instant, he expected
to see Osgood leap from the wall in wild rebellion; but Osgood
did not move. His face was turned to the wall, held close, so that
Gillespie could see only the back of the head. For ten minutes,
Osgood did not move, nor give any sign of fatigue or tension.
With each passing minute, Gillespie expected action: a fall or a
cry of pain; but after ten minutes, he watched Osgood as if
Osgood were an athlete displaying his virtuosity. Gillespie became fascinated by the spectacle; his curiosity submerged his
anxiety. With a remote calculation, he tried to compute time
until Osgood would fall; he did not prepare himself to jump to
Osgood's assistance. Osgood did not show weakness until almost
fifteen minutes after he had been braced into his position; then
his left leg began to shake. Gillespie watched the quivering leg
as if it were the head of a boxer under blows; he was not surprised
when the quivering stopped. Osgood stood firm for twenty minutes altogether. Then, with no warning, while Gillespie was looking away, while the Lieutenant was examining papers on his desk,

and while Johnson had turned away to shrug his shoulders at Sgt. Cann, Osgood fell backwards. He made no sound as he fell. He straightened out as he fell, and his head hit the floor first; the floor shook with the impact. Gillespie looked down, paralyzed; for a moment no one moved. Then Johnson turned to look down; the Lieutenant shook his head slightly.

"He's all right," the Lieutenant said. "He'll get up by himself."

Gillespie, feeling drained of all power, stood rigidly. He watched Osgood's body shake in a sudden spasm; he watched Osgood slowly raise his head. Osgood set his right hand behind him and braced himself into a sitting position, shaking his head with his eyes closed.

"You can get up now," Sgt. Cann said suddenly. His voice was very loud in the quiet room.

"That's right," Johnson said eagerly. "Get up now!" He was looking down at Osgood, staring, eyes wide open. "Get up!" he said again. Gillespie turned to look at him, feeling a horror of what he might see: Johnson's back was toward him, but Johnson was trembling. Beyond Johnson, Gillespie could see Osgood slowly rising to his feet; he stood up slowly, swaying drunkenly, but his eyes were open, moving purposefully in the exhausted face.

"All right," Osgood said. "I'm up now. What do you want now?"

"We want you to stand at ease, Osgood," the Lieutenant said smoothly. "I'll ask you two questions."

"I still don't know anything," Osgood said. "And I'm still strong."

"That may be," the Lieutenant continued. He held Osgood's attention with his smile. "But you should listen to my questions before you answer." The Lieutenant paused, as if out of politeness, waiting for Osgood to speak; but Osgood only looked, fixing his eyes on the Lieutenant's smile. "I'll go on then," the Lieutenant said. "First question: did this man Gillespie put that drawing on the wall? You would do well to tell the truth now, Osgood; the truth will come out eventually, you know."

"I didn't see anything," Osgood answered. "But I can't speak for anyone else: why don't you ask Gillespie?"

"You're sure, Osgood?"

"I didn't see anything."

"Second question: did you make that drawing?"

"No."

The Lieutenant opened his mouth to speak, but before he could get the words out, Sgt. Cann stepped in front of him, past the desk.

"You see, Lieutenant?" he said. "Why waste time with him? Let's let Johnson work him over for a while."

"One moment, Sergeant" the Lieutenant said. "I think you're right, but before we do anything further, I have one more thing to say to this man." He looked up at Osgood. "I'm giving you this chance," he said. "If Gillespie made the drawing, as we think he might have done, you will gain nothing by concealing your knowledge. Gillespie's no great friend of yours anyway."

"I don't know anything," Osgood said flatly. "And I don't need you to tell me that Gillespie is no friend of mine. What do you want now?"

"Nothing, Osgood," the Lieutenant said. "Nothing right now; I'll talk to you again later. Johnson!"

"Here I am, sir."

"You will take this man Osgood into the next room; I don't want to see him again until he is more tractable: is that clear?"

"I understand, sir. I think I can manage it."

"You seem quite sure of yourself, Johnson. Are you sure you understand my requirements?"

"I know what to do," Johnson answered. "I've learned a lot tonight, sir."

"Then you may proceed," the Lieutenant said. "We'll be right here." The Lieutenant sat back in his chair to watch as Johnson directed Osgood through the door into the back room. Gillespie, feeling that no one was watching him, looked toward the door; as Osgood went through, he saw a muscle in Osgood's cheek twitching: the motion moved from the jaw to the ear, in a comprehensive signal. As the door closed, a cry formed on Gillespie's lips; for an

98

instant, he thought of retracting all his actions with one sentence: but the door closed before he could summon his voice. Gillespie looked down at the Lieutenant, but he could say nothing to him: the Lieutenant was playing with the pencil, grinning as he inspected the trademark. Through the closed door, Gillespie could hear Johnson's voice:

"Right over there," the voice said. "Against that wall."

With an expression of mild amusement, the Lieutenant looked past Gillespie at Sgt. Cann.

"I like to listen," he said. "It's possible to learn a great deal by listening."

"It sounds all right," the Sergeant said. "It sounds as if Johnson knows what he's doing."

"I think so," the Lieutenant said. "Johnson is learning very rapidly; I think he understands his duties now." The Lieutenant looked up at Gillespie. "Do you agree with me, Gillespie?"

"I don't know, sir," Gillespie said in a low voice. "I'm not qualified."

"Indeed you're not," the Lieutenant answered. He laughed a little, and then as the idea caught him, he laughed harder. "Indeed you're not! My!" the Lieutenant gasped. "I believe you've caught the essence of the matter." The Lieutenant turned his head as Johnson's voice came again through the closed door.

"Don't move," the voice said. "Stand steady!"

"He seems to be warming to his work," the Lieutenant said. "Does it sound so to you, Sergeant?"

"Something's happening," the Sergeant said. "Maybe we'll get some results now."

The Lieutenant leaned backwards in his chair, listening; but for a time there were no more sounds from the room. For almost three minutes, there were no sounds but the sounds of chairs and breathing. Then Johnson's voice came through the door: the waspishness was gone in a wild urgency.

"Stand steady! Stand steady!"

Gillespie, standing tensely, heard the sound of feet moving rapidly, scuffling on the floor of the next room. The Lieutenant, calm as he heard the voice, jumped to his feet when he heard the scuffle. He turned quickly; reaching for the pistol he carried at his belt, he opened the door. Gillespie stepped to his left to look past the Lieutenant, but before he reached a position where he could see, he heard Johnson's voice, choking a little, but very loud:

"It's all right, sir. Everything's under control."

Through the open door, Gillespie could see Johnson, legs spread, standing over Osgood: Osgood was on his knees in front of Johnson, holding himself up with his right hand, rubbing his forehead with his left hand. In the bright light, Gillespie could see Osgood's lower lip caught up between the opposing rows of teeth; a line of blood was forming at the corner of Osgood's mouth, running from the slashed lip.

"What happened?" the Lieutenant asked. He stepped into the room, but with his right hand he gestured to Sgt. Cann to stay back.

"He wouldn't stand," Johnson said. "The son of a bitch wouldn't stand."

"And you took corrective measures?" the Lieutenant asked.

"I took care of this one," Johnson said. He lifted his right hand, showing the pistol held firmly by the barrel.

"I see," the Lieutenant said. "Do you think you can continue?"

"I'll take care of this one," Johnson answered. "I know how to take care of him now."

"You're sure?" the Lieutenant asked.

"I'm sure, sir. I know what's to be done, sir."

"All right, Johnson," the Lieutenant said. "See that you don't break anything." He stepped back, closing the door behind him. "Get back!" he said to Gillespie. "Stand away from the desk."

Gillespie, unbelieving, watched the Lieutenant sit down at the desk. "You're not going to leave him in there?" he said. "After that?"

"Stand at attention, Gillespie!" the Lieutenant shouted. "And keep your mouth shut! Sgt. Cann! If this man speaks again, stop him!"

"Yes, sir!" the Sergeant said. He stepped up behind Gillespie, moving with quick even steps; Gillespie could feel the Sergeant moving toward him. Sensing a blow, he ducked his head forward and turned, but the Sergeant caught him by the shoulder and spun him around. As Gillespie turned, the Sergeant hammered the heel of his right hand down upon Gillespie's neck, just above the shoulder. Gillespie fell forward across the desk.

"There!" the Sergeant said. "That'll shut him up!"

Through his daze, Gillespie felt the Sergeant catch his collar; he felt a jerk and then he spilled backward off the desk.

"Wake up!" the Sergeant said. "I didn't hit you hard."

Gillespie sagged against the restraining arm, but he wakened with the strokes of the hand against his face; he struggled slowly to his feet. He stood finally alone, and the Sergeant stepped back.

"Is that all right, Lieutenant?" the Sergeant said.

"That will be enough," the Lieutenant said. "Don't hit him again."

"I wanted to loosen him," the Sergeant said. "That's all I wanted to do."

"You were successful enough," the Lieutenant said. "Now leave him alone."

Gillespie, hearing the Lieutenant's voice, looked up. The room spun before him, but as he watched, his vision stabilized: the Lieutenant's face came into focus; he noticed that the Lieutenant's eyes were blue. Before he could straighten the impression, he heard another series of sounds from the next room: feet scuffling, a cry, a blow. The sounds seemed to return as echoes, beating against Gillespie's ears, but he could not move: his eyes lost their focus again; he saw the Lieutenant move but he could not see the whole motion. He saw a motion fused with its reeling background; he leaned forward and rested his body against the desk. Through his confusion, he saw the Sergeant move past him, following the Lieutenant through the door; he heard the Lieutenant's voice, shouting, bloated and vast with rage.

"Drop it!" he heard the Lieutenant call. "Drop it goddammit! Drop it now!"

Gillespie looked up across the desk to the door, but the Sergeant stood on the sill, blocking the view; realizing only disaster at last, Gillespie could see nothing but the Sergeant's back. Painfully, counting each motion as an advance through great distance, Gillespie started to move around the desk, toward the door. As he passed the corner of the desk, he stopped; the Sergeant without looking back, had caught the door and slammed it shut: the door slammed in Gillespie's face like a final answer. Gillespie sat down on the desk and dropped his head in his hands. In the darkness his own hands had created, he could see only the image of Osgood's face; the eyes an unforgiving foreign blue, piercing the darkness, fixed and staring like no other eyes in the world.

CHAPTER TEN

Gillespie waited at the desk for the end of the night's activity; his senses quickened no echoes in his mind: behind his hands, complete darkness prevailed. He did not even hear the Sergeant come back into the office; but he moved with a wild reflex when the Sergeant rapped his right shoulder.

"Get up," the Sergeant said. "Get up and get going."

Gillespie slid from the desk, turning his head to look at the door. "I'll go," he said slowly. "But what happened in there?"

The Sergeant caught him by the shoulder and straightened him; with no sign of emotion in his face, he swept his left arm, backhand, smacking the back of the hand against Gillespie's cheek.

"No questions," the Sergeant said flatly. "Johnson's been hurt by that friend of yours. Now get going; we're going back to the barracks."

Gillespie jumped into motion; he walked before the Sergeant, stepping rapidly. Outside, in the cold night air, he walked faster; behind him, he heard the Sergeant coming on. Just outside the barracks, Gillespie stumbled and fell, but he caught himself before the Sergeant could reach him.

"I'm sorry," he said to the Sergeant. "I'm all right."

The Sergeant opened the big outside door and followed Gillespie into the hall; he closed the door behind him but he did not turn on the houselights; he snapped off the flashlight when he went inside. He caught Gillespie in the hall and backed him up against a wall. Gillespie could feel the Sergeant's hot animal breath break against his face.

"I'm going to tell you something now," the Sergeant said. "And I want you to remember it. You hear me, Gillespie?"

"I can hear you," Gillespie said, nodding his head in the dark.

"You're to keep your mouth shut, Gillespie. Don't talk to

anyone about what's happened tonight; we'll talk to you to-morrow."

"All right, Sergeant," Gillespie said dully. "I'll be quiet."

"Don't make any mistakes, Gillespie; this is a serious matter."

Gillespie felt the Sergeant move away; the hot breath fell away from his face, leaving a sour smell in the air. Gillespie looked down in the darkness, wondering idly whether he had smelled liquor on the Sergeant's breath; he thought about the smell of whiskey as he listened to the Sergeant open the inside door. The Sergeant snapped the flashlight on again and showed Gillespie a path of light to the door.

"Hurry up," the Sergeant said.

The door closed behind Gillespie with a sound more solid than any he remembered; the wire did not rattle in the frame. Without thinking, Gillespie started across the room, stepping over the sleeping prisoners. He touched the third man he tried to pass and he stumbled against a fourth; both woke with him and sat up cursing.

"What the hell," said one. "Where are you going, for Christ's sake!" said the other.

Gillespie mumbled and stepped back; the complaints seemed unanswerable. He turned slowly and went back to the door. He remained standing for almost a minute, slowly calculating ways of reaching his blanket; but he could think of no way: instead of seeing the darkness of the big room, he saw the brightly lighted office, lit up for visitors somewhere outside in the night. Finally, with a sigh, he sank down to the floor. He moved slowly across the floor, squirming from hips to hands against the cold surface, until he was past the door; then he set his back against the wall and closed his eyes: there was no transition from darkness to darkness. He saw no more with his eyes open than with his eyes closed.

It was only two hours until the room was wakened; during that time, Gillespie managed to sleep at intervals. He had no nightmares and he had no dreams but he was glad when he heard movement in the hall; he stood up before anyone else in the room. He looked beyond the light for Sgt. Cann, but he saw an unfamiliar face; he looked around the big room, searching the darkness, and even the room seemed unfamiliar. His body ached. He was very sleepy. As he went out through the opened doors, he closed his mind against all his memories.

Gillespie moved mechanically through the morning. He allowed only a few impressions to reach him: the cold wind, the spongy ground, the blue sky. He did not marvel at the blue sky, although it was the first clear day he had seen for a month; there were no clouds anywhere. After breakfast, he worked quietly; he did not ask himself any questions; and he did not miss Lt. Camber and Sgt. Cann: he held himself suspended from his corruption. He shut up his mind against all the world.

Until noon he was successful. At noon, the little Italian, Nicoletti, cornered him in the latrine, where he had gone to conceal himself from the eyes of the company. Nicoletti called loudly from the door to the latrine.

"Hey Gillespie!"

Gillespie turned his back as he heard Nicoletti approach; the light footsteps had a marching sound, like a regiment in review, on the stone floor.

"I've got news," Nicoletti said. "Jesus have I got the news!" His bald head bobbed in the bright light. "And I'll tell it without asking," Nicoletti went on. "Do you want to hear it?"

"Do we need any news?" Gillespie asked. "I didn't come here for news."

"I know, I know," Nicoletti said. "You probably know it already; but do you know where the Lieutenant is? Or the Sergeant? That's my news; that's what I know." Nicoletti looked up, grinning, so that the corners of his eyes were folded under laughing eyelids.

Gillespie, with a slow and painful movement, drew his right hand across his eyes; he waited for the momentary darkness that came with his hand, and he enjoyed it as it passed. "I don't know, Nick," he said quietly. "Why don't you tell me?"

"They're with the Colonel; they've been there all morning."

"And why are they there, Nick? Did you hear about that? Do you know all about it now so that you can tell me?"

"That's all I know for certain," Nicoletti said. "I could tell you what I heard, though." He moved slowly closer to Gillespie; he reached up and whispered in Gillespie's ear. "I've heard one of the guards was hurt last night; it's just a rumor I've heard." Nicoletti stepped back, not grinning any more; he looked up at Gillespie, withdrawing his eagerness into his curiosity. "And I thought you might be able to tell me something about that," he went on. "I saw you leave the barracks last night with that new guard."

"And you think I might have gotten the guard?"

"O no!" Nicoletti said. "I thought you might know who did; that's all. That's all I meant, Gillespie."

"I know," Gillespie said with a wave of his hand. With sudden irritation he added: "Why don't you go now, Nicoletti? I've had your news." Gillespie set his eyes on Nicoletti's bald head. "You with your news," Gillespie said angrily. "You with your news, and not knowing anything; go on! Leave me alone: get out now!"

Nicoletti jumped back, astonished and hurt; at the door, he paused, as he saw that Gillespie had not moved. "What's the matter with you?" Nicoletti asked. He touched his hand to the doorknob, in preparation, but he did not move.

Gillespie looked across the room, directing his stare like a line thrown across rough water in a storm; he saw Nicoletti as if he had never seen him before; he passed his hand over his eyes again and spoke more quietly. "I don't know, Nick," he said. "I'm sorry I talked to you that way."

"That's all right," Nicoletti said nervously from the door. "Think nothing of it."

"Come on back a minute, then," Gillespie said. His own voice came back to him like an echo from a remote mountain, enriched and vigorous with meanings he had not intended. He looked down from Nicoletti's bald head to the shy nervous face below it; he searched the face for a benevolence he could not believe, but he could not determine whether he saw it or not. "Come on back a minute, Nick," he said again. He watched as Nicoletti regret-

106

fully abandoned the door and moved hesitantly toward him. "Do you want to know what happened last night, Nick?" Gillespie asked. "I could tell you."

"You don't have to tell me," Nicoletti answered. "But I'll listen."

"All right, Nick, I'll tell you: a guard was hurt last night and I was there."

"And did you do it?" Nicoletti asked ferociously. He stepped back as he spoke, as if he feared a blow; but he stopped as he saw Gillespie standing as before.

"But that's all I can tell you," Gillespie said. "I was told not to tell any more, or even talk at all. You understand, Nick?"

"Who did it then?" Nicoletti asked eagerly. "If you didn't do it, who did?"

Gillespie shook his head, not in negation; as if puzzled. "Why I don't know, Nick. I haven't made up my mind about that."

"You don't know?" Nicoletti said incredulously. He stepped back indignantly toward the door. "Are you kidding me?"

"I said I haven't made up my mind yet, Nick!"

"But you saw it done!" Nicoletti said angrily. "You said you saw it!"

"I'm sorry, Nick. I've told you all I know."

"Well, all right then," Nicoletti said. He stepped back again, rubbing the belt of hair that grew above his ears. "I have to go fix my blanket," he said uncertainly. "I think I'd better go tend to it."

"All right, Nick; I won't stop you."

"I'll see you, Gillespie."

"Sure, Nick. You know where to find me."

CHAPTER ELEVEN

Gillespie was relieved when he saw Sgt. Cann enter the barracks before the work call in the afternoon. Gillespie was pleased to see a familiar face among all the new strangers; he started to move toward the door before the Sergeant called. When he heard his name, he answered eagerly.

"Gillespie?"

"Here I am, Sergeant."

Gillespie presented himself at the wire door. "I'm ready, Sergeant," he said.

The Sergeant opened the door for him without speaking, and followed him out the big outside door. Gillespie stopped outside, without turning, while the Sergeant set the locks. "We're going to the office," the Sergeant said firmly. "You know where it is."

There was no one in the office when the Sergeant opened the door. "Go on in," the Sergeant said. "We'll wait here."

The room was very cold. There was a sifting of grey ashes on the floor beneath the stove, powdered in the crevices of the new flooring. Without being told, Gillespie moved toward the desk; beyond the desk, the door to the inner room was closed. Gillespie could see the latch set between the door and the frame; he shuddered and turned from the door to face the Sergeant.

"I have something to say to you, Sergeant," Gillespie said. He looked down at his feet, amazed at his calmness, but pleased with his resolution. As he thought about the night before with its horrors, he could make a pleasant comparison with his present state; he was sure of his condition.

"I'm not interested," the Sergeant answered in a cold voice. "I haven't asked you any questions."

Gillespie looked up in astonishment. "What's the matter?" he asked. "I've got to talk to you, Sergeant!"

"I don't think you have anything to say to me," the Sergeant said.

"But I do," Gillespie said anxiously. "It's a matter of great importance, Sergeant; I've been thinking about it all day."

"I don't want to hear it," the Sergeant said. "I don't want to have anything to do with you."

Gillespie watched as the Sergeant turned to him; he was satisfied to see awakening interest in the Sergeant's face. "Will you listen now, Sergeant?"

The Sergeant looked Gillespie up and down; he stroked his chin and sat down in his chair at the wall. "So you have a confession," he said. "And what do you have to confess, Gillespie?"

Gillespie smiled involuntarily as he caught the Sergeant's eyes. He remembered his talk with Osgood on the evening before the last interrogation; something of his mood then came back to him: he remembered Osgood's approving smile as he had said that he intended to confess to his actions. The smile came to him from a great distance but in a fierce clarity of memory. Gillespie felt the same sudden beatitude he had known before.

"It's a long story," Gillespie began. "It'll take a little time."

The Sergeant looked at his watch. "We have half an hour," he said. "The Lieutenant won't be here until two o'clock. Go ahead, Gillespie; I'm listening."

"All right, Sergeant." Gillespie paused, as he chose his words; the whole memory of the incident in the Colonel's room came back to him: his mind was perfectly clear. Each incident fell into place in the day's pattern; as he closed his right hand, he could almost feel the weight of the glass from the picture frame compacted with the toilet paper into a solid mass; he remembered the sharp pain he had felt from the cuts in his hand. "First of all," Gillespie continued, "I'll say that it has nothing to do with the drawing on the barracks wall; it's something that has nothing to do with that drawing."

The Sergeant looked up in surprise. "What did you say?"

"I said it had nothing to do with the drawing on the barracks wall: the drawing of the horse in charcoal."

"Then why do you tell me?" the Sergeant asked. His features were drawn tight, as if closed over unrevealed knowledges.

"Because you should know it, Sergeant. It has to do with what happened last night; I know it does." Gillespie looked at the Sergeant, waiting for words, but the Sergeant only looked at him: the Sergeant's face was blank and drawn; his cheekbones showed white through his dark skin.

"It's about a photograph that belongs to the Colonel," Gillespie said. "I want to tell you about that."

"I'm not stopping you, Gillespie," the Sergeant said quietly. "Go right ahead."

"I want to tell you that I broke it," Gillespie said suddenly; and as the words came out, he breathed in deeply: the stale sodden air of the little room worked a cool blessing in his lungs. Gillespie gasped a little.

"I said go ahead," the Sergeant said grimly. "You don't have to stop."

"I'll tell you all about it," Gillespie said breathlessly. Through his exhilaration, he could not see the Sergeant clearly: he saw only a figure poised on the chair, waiting; an intelligence behind a dark face. Gillespie started the story at the beginning, when he and Osgood had started washing the walls of the Colonel's bedroom; after a time, he stopped watching the Sergeant's face: he told his story to his shoes and to the floor. The memories rose to his mind clothed already in the necessary words; he spoke a swift monologue. He spent no more time with the breaking of the picture than with his motives for concealing it; he provided no emphases for the actions he described: no deed was darker than another. It took him fifteen minutes to complete his narrative; and when he finished, he did not raise his head. He stood humble before the Sergeant as before a priest or an executioner. The Sergeant waited for almost thirty seconds before he spoke.

"Is that all, Gillespie?" he asked then. "Do you have anything more to say?"

"That's all, Sergeant. I've told you everything."

"May I ask you a question then?" the Sergeant said. "I'm not quite clear on all of the details."

110

"Anything, Sergeant. I'm glad to be rid of it all."

"Then did you say that you denied breaking the picture to Johnson last night? When you knew that Johnson was sure to blame Osgood for it?"

"That's right, Sergeant. It's all my fault; everything that happened last night was my fault."

"I see," the Sergeant said. "And now you want to make it right to both of them. Is that right?"

"That's what I want to do, Sergeant. I think that's my duty."

Gillespie looked up at the Sergeant; he watched the Sergeant rise from his chair and turn to him; without surprise, Gillespie waited for the Sergeant to speak.

"Then there's something you should know, Gillespie," the Sergeant said. He paused and waited for Gillespie's attention to come to a sharp focus upon him. "Are you listening, Gillespie?"

"I'm listening, Sergeant."

"Then hear this, Gillespie; hear this! Johnson is dead! He died this morning at eleven o'clock! You're too late with your confessions, Gillespie; too late to help anyone!"

Gillespie blinked and shook his head, like a steer under the butcher's hammer. He shook his head three times; the third time, he snapped his head as if to tear it loose from his shoulders. "O no!" he cried. "O my God in heaven!" He stepped back, reeling within the monumental shock; as he turned, his eyes caught Sgt. Cann, standing grimly with his feet set wide apart on the floor. "Is that the truth?" Gillespie called. "Is that the truth, man?"

"I was there when he died," the Sergeant said. "And I heard him say goodbye."

Gillespie turned away; as he bent down, the desk caught his weight; he hooked his body slowly over the edge of the desk. The Sergeant's words rang in his ears, echoed from ear to ear, carrying all the richness of the Sergeant's big voice magnified about them. Slowly Gillespie settled himself on the desk; his body turned him without his volition again toward the Sergeant; Gillespie's eyes opened again to comprehend the Sergeant's accusation.

"Why didn't you tell me before!" Gillespie said. "Why did you

111

let me go on with it? O my God, why didn't you tell me?" Gillespie's words rang out in the room so loudly that he could not hear them; they came back blinding his mind with echoes in the silence that expanded to take them in: Gillespie heard them again and again and he could not stop them. Before his eyes, the figure of the Sergeant was only a figure; the figure changed very slowly, second by second, into an articulated human being. "Why didn't you tell me!" Gillespie shouted again; this time his words had no echoes. The Sergeant jumped with the sound.

"I told you once!" the Sergeant said angrily. "Do you want it changed by different telling?"

"You should have told me earlier," Gillespie said brokenly. Bent by the desk and warped in his agony, Gillespie caught his head in his hands; he swayed slowly from the hips, weaving his torso from side to side.

"You've no complaints anyway, Gillespie," the Sergeant said. "What right have you to complain: with one man dead and another to hang after trial? Do you hear me, Gillespie?"

"I know it, I know it," Gillespie said. "It's all over now."

"That's right, Gillespie; so don't complain. Be quiet; be a man!"

Gillespie quivered with each word. In a clear region of his mind, he saw that he should weep; but he could not channel his grief into tears: the edges of his eyes were dry. He saw very clearly that the bitter salt would help him, but he could not find his justification. The act of Osgood appeared as an act of his own, so that he felt responsibility rather than the consequential sorrow. He was not meant for the chief mourner; he was meant for the gallows before his friend. He thought with amazement of what the Sergeant had said: everything had happened to others; he alone remained unscathed. He dropped his hands from his head and looked up at the Sergeant.

"What can I do?" he asked. "What can I do now to help him?"

"You can be quiet now," the Sergeant said savagely. "You can at least keep the peace."

"But it was all my fault; I showed you that. Nobody knew what I was doing; I had everybody fooled: that's why there was trouble. Can't you see that, Sergeant?"

"It's not my job to see that," the Sergeant answered. "I never had a chance to know that poor devil Johnson. All I know is that he was doing his duty, a nice little guy: now be quiet, Gillespie!"

"But I have to show you," Gillespie said. "It's very important that I show you."

"I said be quiet! I mean it now."

Gillespie saw the Sergeant step toward him. Gillespie did not move; with a sudden hope, he looked for the Sergeant to strike him; he anticipated the blow as the beginning of his expiation: but the Sergeant stopped, hesitant, opening and closing his hands, and then stood staring at Gillespie.

"Do you hear me, Gillespie? I want you to be quiet now until the Lieutenant comes; that's all I want from you, Gillespie." The Sergeant turned quickly to his chair; as he sat down, Gillespie straightened himself on the desk: he tried to remember all he knew of Lt. Camber. Seeing that Sgt. Cann would do nothing because he comprehended nothing, Gillespie directed his hopes toward Lt. Camber; he summoned up all the images at his command. But before he could manage a summation, he remembered the Lieutenant's blue eyes; and the blue eyes chilled him: his hopes disappeared in the memory that fitted perfectly across his memory of Osgood's eyes. Gillespie could not pass the eyes and the image that grew around them. Gillespie settled himself on the edge of the desk; he watched the door to the hall. He focussed the confusion in his mind upon the plain and palpable fact of the door; it held steady for him, the only steady thing in his world, while he waited for the Lieutenant to come.

CHAPTER TWELVE

Lt. Camber, with his trousers newly pressed, with creases in the sleeves of his shirt, and wearing the outer freshness of a new shave, entered the office without knocking: he closed the door behind him with a sharp gesture of his hand and wrist; his heels hit the floor with a precise leathern click. Gillespie, having heard his steps in the hall, was standing in front of the desk, carefully in the position of attention.

"Attention!" Sgt. Cann called, standing himself.

"Stand at ease!" the Lieutenant called.

The Lieutenant seated himself behind the desk and Gillespie turned to face him; Gillespie watched the Lieutenant's face with the utmost care. He was a little surprised to see the Lieutenant appear so fresh and ready; but he built his hopes on the Lieutenant's impassivity, forgetting unhappy possibilities as he read kindness and perception and sympathy in the Lieutenant's face.

"Well Gillespie," the Lieutenant began. "How are you today?"

"I'm all right, sir," Gillespie said slowly.

"I should imagine you would be, Gillespie; you at least are still at large." The Lieutenant leaned back in his chair. "Do you agree, Gillespie?"

Before Gillespie could answer, Sgt. Cann stepped up to the desk, raising his right hand for attention. "Sir," the Sergeant began, "I have something to tell you."

"Certainly, Sergeant," the Lieutenant said in the same voice as before. "Tell it."

"Yes, sir," the Sergeant said. "It concerns this man Gillespie; it's something Gillespie told me before you got here."

"Just now?"

"He finished just before you came, sir. It has to do with what happened last night."

114

"Just a moment then, Sergeant," the Lieutenant said. "Perhaps Gillespie could tell it himself; how about that, Sergeant?"

"I thought I could tell it quicker," the Sergeant said. "Whatever you want, sir."

"I think I should like to hear it from Gillespie," the Lieutenant said. "No slur upon you, Sergeant, you understand."

"O yes, sir. I understand."

"Then speak up, Gillespie!" the Lieutenant said. "Tell me what you told the Sergeant."

"It's a long story," Gillespie said. "I guess I'd better start at the beginning."

"By all means, yes. Start at the beginning, Gillespie; the Colonel won't be here until two-thirty."

"Then the Colonel's coming!" Gillespie said. "Will you let me talk to him, Lieutenant?" Gillespie bent forward over the desk, bending all his powers with his body upon the Lieutenant's surprise. "I have to see him, Lieutenant!"

"Stand back, please!" the Lieutenant said. "You must remain at attention while you're addressing an officer." The Lieutenant looked up, bobbing his head, as if to mark time to his own commands; his blue eyes caught Gillespie and drove him back.

"O yes, sir," Gillespie said. "Only I must see the Colonel, sir. It's very important."

"You may put your mind at ease then, Gillespie; the Colonel is coming for the one purpose of seeing and talking to you. I'll say something about that later; now, your story."

Hurrying, and thinking beyond the Lieutenant to the dignity of the Colonel, Gillespie repeated his story; he found the phrases familiar. It was like telling a lewd story, time-honored, and rounded to perfection by selective repetition. Everything came back. As the story progressed, Gillespie found again a part of the beatitude he had known as he had planned his confession; the recital of simple events diverted his mind from the consequences of the events. Johnson appeared again as an impersonal dignitary who enjoyed shaving a bar of soap; Osgood as the fierce and honorable man he had always been. The murder was lost in lucidity.

115

After Gillespie finished, the Lieutenant remained silent; he found his comforting pencil and examined the trademark.

"And is that all, Gillespie? Are you quite finished now?"

"That's the whole story, sir," Gillespie said with dignity. "It's the truth as I know it, sir; and it was as bad as it sounds, sir."

"It's an interesting story, Gillespie," the Lieutenant said. "I presume you wish to see the Colonel so that you can tell him the same story?"

"That's what I have to do, sir," Gillespie said.

"I'll put it before the Colonel for you," the Lieutenant said. "Though you understand I am not myself interested in it; do you realize that there may be consequences?"

"I don't care about that, sir! I want to do what I can for Osgood; though it's too late for Johnson."

"That's enough, Gillespie! I advise you not to think about that: the crime has been committed. You can't expect to change that."

"I know, sir! I want to tell my story and take the consequences."

"All right, Gillespie. Now, no more of this. Before the Colonel comes, there are a few things I must tell you." The Lieutenant juggled the pencil between his fingers, and then set it up between his two hands, the point set in the left forefinger, the eraser set in the palm of the right hand; he examined the pencil as if it were a message in code laid out before his eyes. While he watched the pencil, the Lieutenant spoke in a soft voice. "First of all, Gillespie, you must watch your conduct; the Colonel permits no liberties: stand at attention always! As to what happened last night, we want you to tell the truth; no more. I want you to remember that your friend Osgood provoked us in a manner which could properly have been punished with extreme severity. The only pity is that we did not so punish him. We will have to wait for that until after his trial. Now these aren't instructions; I want you to understand that these are only the dictates of decency. Do you understand that, Gillespie?" The Lieutenant opened his hands and the pencil dropped to the desk, clattered, and rolled to a stop against a bottle of ink. "I want you to be clear in your mind, Gillespie."

While the Lieutenant had spoken, Gillespie listened closely; he waited for a word of anger or condemnation: for a moment, he comprehended only the outer meanings of what the Lieutenant had said. Understanding that he had time to design his anger, Gillespie hesitated; he looked once at the Lieutenant's eyes and was appalled: suddenly he was overwhelmed by the hypocrisy.

"The dictates of decency!" he said. "I don't understand you, sir!"

"You're to understand that I've said what I mean," the Lieutenant answered. "There's no blood on my hands, Gillespie."

"And will you let me tell my story, sir? I think the Colonel should hear it, sir."

"You will talk to the Colonel and answer his questions, Gillespie; at this time more than any other, you will observe all the proprieties."

"Yes, sir," Gillespie answered. "But I'll tell my story, sir; I see my duty, sir!"

"You will answer questions, Gillespie!" the Lieutenant said angrily. He stood up slowly, rebuilding his dignity with each inch of elevation; he stood finally with his hands on his hips, leaning forward across the desk. "By God, Gillespie," he said, "I won't tolerate any more of this; no more!" The Lieutenant glared across the desk at Gillespie, and then sank suddenly into his chair again. As Gillespie watched, he saw the Lieutenant's shoulders shake; the tremor worked upward. The Lieutenant reached up suddenly and passed his right hand across his forehead, and as his hand fell toward the table, the Lieutenant closed the hand and swept it violently across the desk, striking the inkbottle from the table in a flat arc. The inkbottle struck the wall beside the desk and bounced to the floor. Gillespie watched as the inkbottle teetered on a corner and then slowly tipped over on its side. "Well, pick it up!" the Lieutenant said. "Pick it up, Gillespie: are you blind?"

With a swift quiet gesture, Gillespie stooped over and picked up the inkbottle and set it on the desk.

"Don't make me speak again, Gillespie," the Lieutenant said wearily. "My God! Can't you see I've been through a great deal this last day and night? Sgt. Cann, take this man into the back room and keep him quiet there until I call you."

Working within a catastrophic disappointment, Gillespie stepped toward the corner of the desk; he watched the Lieutenant, who held his head down, propped on the heel of his right hand: the Lieutenant was curling the fingers of his hand, as if to relieve a pain. Gillespie opened the door to the back room himself; he was surprised to find the door unlocked. He turned to hold the door for the Sergeant, and as he moved the Lieutenant spoke again.

"I want you out of my sight for a while," the Lieutenant said quietly. "Lord! Sometimes I can't believe I'm the proper owner of a home with three bedrooms and two baths: go on Gillespie! I'm too tired to look at you."

Uneasily, Gillespie slipped past the door. He wondered why the room had not been sealed: it could have been done, he thought, if not for evidence, at least for a memorial. He decided bitterly that it was fitting for him to return to the place of his disaster; the circle began to close, leaving only a narrow arc yet remaining to be comprehended. As he heard the Sergeant come through the door, Gillespie tried to imagine what a house with three bedrooms and two baths looked like; but as the door closed, he forgot the problem: he went to the center of the room and waited; and when he heard the Colonel enter the outer office with an accompaniment of salutes and greetings, he did not raise his head; nor did he look at Sgt. Cann. Caught up in the circle of the higher powers, he did not heed the presence of the Sergeant; and the Sergeant said nothing to him. Without fear, Gillespie listened to the sound of voices from the next room. Without anger at the Lieutenant, he fashioned from the remnants of his resolution a new hope: he did not after all know the Colonel; anything was possible. He thought of Osgood, and in that memory he found forces to guide him in his efforts at assistance. As he waited to be called, he anticipated the familiar tremblings in his left leg, but they did not come; the firmness in his leg worked upward to his mind. When the Lieutenant knocked on the door and called, Gillespie stepped forward confidently, like the groom at a wedding.

118

The Colonel was seated in the Lieutenant's chair, behind the Lieutenant's desk, when Gillespie entered the room: the Colonel's face was red as remembered and sharp as ever. Gillespie stood straight before the Colonel for a full minute before the Colonel spoke.

"I am here today on serious business," the Colonel began gravely. "A murder, next to rape the worst of crimes, has been committed in my command. It is my duty to see that the guilty man is punished properly; and in the interests of that duty, I will ask you certain questions, Gillespie, and deliver three lectures. Lieutenant Camber, am I right in believing that this man did not see the actual crime?"

"Yes, sir, you're right, sir. He was here in the office with me at the time it happened."

"Very good," the Colonel said. "Now, Gillespie, the first question: did you observe the prisoner Osgood enter the inner room accompanied by the guard Johnson? Answer yes or no and no more than either, please."

"Why yes, sir," Gillespie began.

"That will be enough, Gillespie. Second question: did anyone enter that room before Lt. Camber?"

"No, sir."

"Very good, Gillespie. Those are the questions. Now, in the interests of a better personal understanding of this affair, I will listen to what you have described to Lt. Camber as your story; but since I have had that story from the Lieutenant already, I wish you to be brief: what have you to say for yourself, Gillespie?"

Gillespie was astonished; from the first word the Colonel had spoken, Gillespie had felt himself buried under a foreign and unpleasant comprehension of his actions: the Colonel had overpowered him. He could not find his tongue. For almost thirty seconds, as he felt his own inadequacy and the Colonel's control of every thing and every man in the room, he tried to form his thoughts.

"Speak up, man," the Colonel said finally. "Surely you understand that I have other affairs than this to tend to."

"Yes, sir," Gillespie said hurriedly. "It's only that I want to help

Osgood, sir," he finished awkwardly. He looked down at the Colonel, hoping desperately for understanding.

"I expect so," the Colonel said drily. "However, I find your present attitude hard to understand in view of your past actions, Gillespie."

"That's it!" Gillespie said suddenly, excitedly. "That's just it, sir. I want to explain to you about Osgood, sir. I want to tell you why it wasn't his fault, sir; yes; that's it, sir!"

"Then do it quickly, Gillespie; that's what I asked for, you know."

"Yes, sir," Gillespie said. "What I want to say is that it wasn't Osgood's fault at all; he couldn't help himself. And it wasn't Johnson's fault either. It was my fault, sir!" Gillespie almost smiled. "That's what I've been meaning to say all along, sir."

"You may continue," the Colonel said.

"You see, sir, Osgood was right all along: he told me the right thing to do; I should have come out with it right away and taken my chances. And last night, after I lied to Johnson, Osgood was caught; he was caught because he wouldn't say anything for himself: he wouldn't fight back at me, sir! He wouldn't fight back at me when I was the attacker, sir! Do you see that sir?"

"Go on," the Colonel said. "I'm listening quite carefully."

"And that's my story," Gillespie said quietly. "I think Osgood was defending himself from me, sir; it was I who got him in the trouble, and he could never forget that he knew how to fight. I can't think of anything more! Do you understand, sir?"

"And have you nothing more to say, Gillespie?" the Colonel asked.

Gillespie nodded his head. "That's all, sir; I want to help as much as I can now."

"I see," the Colonel said. "Perhaps now it's time for my lectures; if you will listen carefully, Gillespie, I will proceed."

"O I'll listen, sir! I'll listen!"

"Indeed you will," the Colonel said. "To be sure, you will!" The Colonel looked down once at his hands, folded and quiescent on the desktop. "The first lecture concerns discipline, Gillespie; discipline considered in its general implications, and in its prac-

120

tical applications to this crime. I am particularly concerned that you hear and understand this lecture, Gillespie; are you listening now?"

"Yes, sir!"

"The basic fact relating to discipline is its necessity," the Colonel began; "and the basic law of discipline is that it shall be rigorous. I have adjusted my life to this fact and this law: I know my relation to both. Is that quite clear, Gillespie?"

"Yes, sir! I do understand you, sir!"

"The practical application of my knowledge to this crime is just as clear, Gillespie. When I saw that my photograph had disappeared from its appointed place, on the day you were working in my quarters, I was able to understand the implications of the facts which I observed. Johnson was in charge of the detail, and consequently of the house, the men, and my personal belongings; the absence of the picture revealed a dereliction of duty for which Johnson was responsible. I therefore relieved him of his position; and assigned all the men on that detail to special work of an unpleasant nature. Because I also comprehend the nature of justice, I assigned Johnson to this company in the prison, so that he could work out a proper adjustment of his guilt to the specific guilt of the man who had broken the picture. Only a vindictive and savage crime could have unhinged the operation of this plan; and that crime has now been committed. Such a crime can never be forgiven; and I shall not forgive it, Gillespie! Do you, Lt. Camber, think I have made myself clear?"

"Yes, sir," the Lieutenant answered. "Abundantly clear, sir."

"And you, Gillespie; have I made myself clear to you?"

Gillespie looked down but he could not speak; his lips moved but no words came.

"I think I have," the Colonel said with cold finality. "Now, my second lecture. Before I begin, I shall say that this will be painful to me; as I trust it will be painful to you: I cannot look complacently upon evil. I will speak of you now, Gillespie, although I find it difficult: you are a vile creature, Gillespie. Your friend will die because of you, and in your place; the rope will find him as surely as we are here now in this room. And justice will be

121

served when he hangs: he has murdered a fellow man; he is marked with the mark of Cain. You, Gillespie, escape unscathed: it makes me wonder at our system, Gillespie! Your safety almost destroys my belief!" The Colonel lifted his right hand above the desk, closed it in a fist, and crashed it down on the table. "And you cannot answer!" the Colonel said triumphantly. "You know I am right, Gillespie! Speak if you can!"

Rigid, stiff, running with sweat, Gillespie looked toward the wall: the wall was blank before him. "I just want to help," he said. "I'll take the consequences."

The Colonel snapped himself straight in his chair. "But don't you see, Gillespie," he began slowly, "don't you see, Gillespie, that there will be no consequences? There will be no consequences!" the Colonel shouted.

Suddenly, showing embarrassment, the Colonel subsided into the chair; he coughed once, and then was silent. His shoulders rose and fell with the wild leap of his lungs. His thick chest, expanding with air and oratory, filled his shirt, drew the buttons tight; for almost a minute no one spoke. The Colonel watched Gillespie, at first with anger inexpressible, and then slowly with comprehension: his lips drew tight across his teeth.

"No!" said the Colonel. "It can't be but it is! Lieutenant Camber, look: can it be remorse? Is it remorse that I see in that face?" The Colonel twisted in his chair, commanding the Lieutenant to move with every motion of his own; the Lieutenant stepped slowly forward: his mouth curled over a beginning smile, he held his face with his full reaction in waiting for an indication from the Colonel. He inspected Gillespie's shoes, and then let his eyes move upward to Gillespie's face; he nodded his head twice.

"Why yes, sir!" the Lieutenant said. "I believe it is, sir!" Slowly the Lieutenant permitted his grin to grow; then he laughed, letting the sound roll out into the room. "Why yes, sir," the Lieutenant said again. He tossed his head back and laughed. His throat moved, shuttling with laughter.

"Lieutenant!" the Colonel thundered. "Stop that! I order you to stop laughing! Have you gone insane, Lieutenant?"

The Lieutenant's laughter stopped abruptly; he looked down at the Colonel: his mouth fell open and then snapped shut.

"Why yes, sir," the Lieutenant began. "Of course, sir."

"I said stop laughing," the Colonel said loudly. "Your conduct is incredible, Lieutenant; it is insupportable. Are you unable to perceive the gravity of this situation?"

"O I'm sorry, sir," the Lieutenant said. "I couldn't help it, sir."

The Colonel watched as the Lieutenant stepped back; then the Colonel turned again to Gillespie, driving the force of his eyes upon him. "Now, Gillespie," he said. "Do you see what you have done? Even my officers are corrupted. Gillespie, look at me; no, not at the wall, not at the door nor the desk; at me, Gillespie. Look! Look!"

Gillespie's head moved obediently; as his head bent, the tears rolled freely down his cheeks, into the corners of his mouth, to penetrate his lips and leave a sediment of salt on his tongue; he closed his eyes and the tears ran on through his darkness. The Colonel's voice came to him through complete darkness, but he heard every word that was spoken to him.

"Gillespie," the Colonel said, "I think perhaps you know it now: there will be no consequences! Neither the picture of my family nor the picture on the barracks wall will touch you; there will be no consequences today, or tomorrow, or on any other day that you will know: do you hear me, Gillespie?"

"I hear you," Gillespie said slowly. "I hear you, sir."

"Then you are prepared, I think, for my last lecture, Gillespie. I had intended one speech for you, but as I see your condition, I think another is in order; a brief lecture on something you should already know, but which you have apparently forgotten: a brief lecture on the position of the soldier at attention is required." The Colonel's voice was dry and uninflected. As if reciting from memory, the Colonel directed his voice into the room. "The position of the soldier at attention is determined by the following orders: the heels will be held together, the feet will be held at a forty-five degree angle. The legs will be held straight, the head up, shoulders back; hands at the seams of the trousers. The soldier will look like a soldier on extremest duty. Now, Gillespie, stand to my order: stand at attention! Stand!"

"Yes, sir," Gillespie said. He could feel the order taking hold in his body; he felt his legs stiffen, his head rise: he looked past the Colonel's head to the door to the inner room. He was confident that he was standing well, but he did not expect applause. He was neither wakeful nor sleepy; his eyes were open but his mind was asleep. He was prepared to stand for a long time if that too should be required of him.